THE
LONG
JOURNEY

Ilse-Dore Pulliam

The Long Journey
by Ilse-Dore Pulliam

Copyright © 2023
All rights reserved.

Photos provided by Ilse-Dore Pulliam

Library of Congress Control Number: 2023937227
International Standard Book Number: 978-1-60126-857-0

Masthof Press
219 Mill Road | Morgantown, PA 19543-9516
www.Masthof.com

TABLE OF CONTENTS

DEDICATED:

As my 50th Anniversary gift
to my husband Gary,
who has always been
a loyal friend,
and my inspiration.

A LONG JOURNEY

It was still snowing outside. I lay in bed dreaming about building a snowman and watching my brothers build their snow castle. The wind whistled and blew large flakes against my window. Our house was old without any heat upstairs. My bedroom was cold, but I was burning up with fever. As long as our doctor was not sure I had scarlet fever, Mother was the only person allowed in my bedroom. Once in a while I would hear my sister or brothers from behind the door ask me how I was feeling. This isolation was not easy for me to understand because I was only three and one half years old.

"Give the girl a hot bath, as hot as she can stand it." I heard our doctor tell mom during his next visit. He looked funny in his ski outfit with hands as cold as ice as he touched me. My tongue was swollen and looked like an oversized raspberry, all the signs of scarlet fever. Only the rash was missing. The hot bath would bring it to the surface, he said before he left. And he was right. After sitting in our old portable metal bathtub I was covered with a red rash all over my chest and back. Now I had to be hospitalized, because scarlet fever was a very contagious disease. This outbreak had already caused many lives, especially children. I hated to leave with Christmas approaching. Mom had to use her skies to take me to the hospital. I cried while she dressed me with two layers of clothing. "Always remember, our heavenly Father loves you and will make you well," she said, wiping her glasses, which she always did after her tears had fogged them up. "Maybe by Christmas you'll be home again."

Finally I was bundled up like a mummy, wrapped in a blanket and tied with a rope to the top of our sled. Mother buckled on her skies, fastened the rope which pulled my sled to her waist belt and we were on our way. It was a clear night with millions of stars in sight. Ice crystals on trees and fences sparkled like pure silver and the air was crisp and cold. At first we went down the village street. It was a smooth ride. But that changed as soon as Mother took a shortcut over snow covered fields and meadows. And I was sure I had fallen off my sled, if I would have not been tied down. From time to time mom turned around to see that it had not flipped over. The wind began to pick up over the open field and it started to snow again. In the dark and Mother being in a hurry, she didn't notice the snow was settling on my face. I tried to free my hands so I could wipe away the snow to breathe better, but I could not pull my arms out of the blanket. I called out to her several times, but the wind and her woolen ski cap prevented her from hearing me. Snow kept getting in my eyes and mouth and as I finally cried out with all the energy I had left, she stopped and turned around. She wiped all the snow off me. To change my position she had to untie me. That became a difficult struggle, because of the wet and frosty rope and her numb fingers. After she asked the Lord for His help, I was soon laying upside down tied back onto the sled. The bumpy journey continued.

Because of my fever I must have lost touch with reality and finally woke up. Sunshine came through a huge window. Dressed with my nightgown and all covered up I found myself lying in a strange bed. I tried to rise, but I couldn't move. My arms seemed to weigh a ton. I could hardly manage to touch my face. I looked around. For as far as I could see, there were children in white beds all around me. Suddenly I remembered my mother telling me about taking me to a hospital. It wasn't long before a nurse came to my bed and sat me on a strange looking bedpan. "So, you are Ilse-Dore, the girl who arrived late last night by, sled," she said and smiled at me. "Your mother will come to visit you next Sunday." Before she left, she gave me some medication, which tasted as bad as it smelled.

During the following days, I was not so sure, if sometimes I was awake or dreaming, I watched children being carried out and replaced with others, and I wondered how many children had been in my bed before me and how long it would be, before I died and being carried out.

But not only the children changed from time to time, it was also the nurses. The new nurse kept looking at me, as if she was blaming me for being ill and she never had a smile or kind word for me. Each time I asked her something, I received no answer, until I finally gave up. After she left, I cried silently under my covers, hoping no one would notice it. Sometimes after she put me on the bedpan, she pulled it out from under me, never bothering to ask if I was finished with my business, and when she combed and braided my hair, she pulled so hard my scalp started to hurt. Since she used the same comb for all of us, head lice had spread. Chairs had been placed in the center aisle of this large room. We had to sit on these chairs a long time, our hair saturated with a strong, awful-smelling solution called Cuprex. With our heads wrapped in turban-style towels, we all looked like miniature white-faced Arabs. The odor alone was enough to make someone faint. Several children had to vomit. I could endure the smell, but I had a problem sitting upright for such a long time. Each time the nurse noticed me almost slipping off the seat, she came, kicking me in my ribs and told me to sit up straight. That day, during dinner, I felt too weak to eat, too worn out to even cry; all I could think and dream of was going home.

One morning I heard church bells ringing near and from far away. I knew it must be Sunday, the day my mother would visit me. A new nurse came to pick me up. She smiled at me and carried me to the corner window of the room. "Your mother is out there," she said kindly. "The window may not be opened, so wave at her, because she cannot hear you." Among a lot of women on the lawn I spotted my mother. There was that painful feeling I had hidden deep inside of me, which I no longer could prevent from surfacing. I no longer cared about being that brave little girl that everyone expected me to be, I wanted my mother to hold me. I started to scream and struggle with the nurse. She got upset with me and put me back to bed, where I cried myself to sleep. The following day I heard, my temperature had risen. This repeated a few more Sundays, until I no longer was allowed to see my mother because of what they called "bad behavior." From that day on, each Sunday, I watched the other children wave at their families while I had to stay in bed. It caused me to develop a certain dislike for nurses, doctors and hospitals. "Here is a letter for you," a nurse said, waking me up. She dropped an envelope on my covers and walked away. I was too young to read, but I noticed my mother's handwriting. I didn't care what it contained, I just knew it was a part of her and I kept holding it. I daydreamed of home, taking a nap on the lawn in the shade of the lilac tree in front of the house. I could hear the buzzing of the bees, watched the butterflies landing quietly and unafraid on the flowers next to me. I felt the summer breeze and listened to the birds building their nest in the nearby cherry tree. That was home, where children laughed instead of crying and where my mother was the only authority. Home was a place where I watched the evening sun painting the sky with stripes of gold, pink and purple. Once more I looked at the letter. I knew my mother loved me and I had not been forgotten. I was sure I had found a perfect hiding place by pushing it into my pillow case. But this happiness only lasted until another nurse found it and took it away.

One morning I woke up and all I could see was fog. I kept rubbing my eyes but the fog would not lift. I sat up to listen. All the familiar sounds around me assured me, I was still in the hospital. First I cried and finally I screamed, "I can't see anything, I am blind!" I thought I was losing my mind, until I felt someone touching me and calming me down. The nurse promised me, she would help. She washed my eyes with some liquid. Objects began to move in the fog, first unidentifiable, but soon I could see the nurse and all twenty-eight beds again. My nightmare had passed, but only to return several more mornings, until it never came back.

The little girl in the bed across the aisle died during one night. Her bed was now occupied by a new girl, named Doris. She was four years older than I. She could turn her fake smiles on and off as if she had an internal switch, her voice was loud and ugly and she talked all day long. Sometimes I was wondering, if she was even sick. Turning my back to her, I acted asleep most of the time and this made her dislike me from the start.

One afternoon I received a package from one of my three godmothers, named Ruth. The nurse helped me to empty it. Out came a large beautiful fairy tale book with a note attached, that she was hoping I was getting well, a banana and a large orange. Those were fruits I had only seen in picture books, because they only grew far beyond the borders of our country. The orange smelled so good, I would have taken a big bite out of it, if the nurse would not have stopped me. She explained to me that it needed to be peeled and as soon as I would have the doctor's permission to eat it, she would tell me. In the meantime everything was being stored in my night chest. Happy, I sank back into my pillow, just knowing someone loved me enough to send me such a treasure.

But my happiness only lasted until the next morning. The nurse pointed at the peelings of both fruits on the floor next to my bed and accused me of being disobedient. By the time I was fully awake and figured out what might have happened, she had thrown the peelings into my wastebasket, cursed me and left. If I only could talk to my mother, I thought, and I cried. Who could have done such a terrible thing? I didn't have to wait long for an answer. It was Doris who stared at me with one of her nasty smiles. Then she had the courage to ask me if I enjoyed the smell of the peelings and laughed. I felt like fighting back, but I was too small and too sick. All I could do was turn around so she could no longer see how hurt I was. Later I daydreamed about the magic powers in my fairy tales and wished she would turn into an ugly green frog, jump around all day and go crazy. I must have fallen asleep because suddenly I woke up, remembering my wish. I looked at her bed, expecting to see a frog. But she was sleeping with the innocent face of an angel. I felt ashamed of what I had wished and glad it had not come true. Maybe she was already sorry for what she had done to me. I decided to be nice to her and forget all about the whole incident.

In the late evening, only the night lights were burning, Doris came to my bed telling me my mother had come to take me home. She picked me up and carried me out to see her. We went down the long hallway and entered a small room. There she sat me on top of a high utility cabinet in front of an open window. "I know you will never tell on me," she said nastily and left. I was too high up to jump and no matter how hard I cried or loud I screamed, no one came to help me.

I did not know how much time had passed. I must have fainted, because I suddenly felt someone slapping me on my back, calling me by my name and brushing the snow off me, which had drifted in through the open window. I was freezing. The nurse was upset with me, believing I had climbed up on the cabinet all on my own. I wanted to explain what had happened, but all I could do was cling to her and utter a few words, shaking all over. She was so mad at me that she put me to bed without changing my wet gown. I was glad to be back under my covers and soon warmed up. But the following day I developed a bad cough and from that day on, felt more ill and weak than I ever had before. When no one was looking, Doris called my name, made an ugly face and stuck her tongue out at me. Watching her through my feverish eyes, I just felt too sick to care.

The weeks that followed I was so ill that my dreams and reality seemed to melt together. Sometimes I thought I heard Christmas carols and watched as the nurses decorated a tree. But I was not able to tell if it was real or not. One morning I woke up and saw a man standing at the foot of my bed, with a bearded face and glasses, making notes and looking at me from time to time. He told the nurse I no longer needed medication, because there was a shortage. I was wondering if he thought I was a hopeless case or I was on my way to recovery. I had now a new sickness that he called pneumonia. I had never heard of such a thing before and I refused to die, especially without my mother being present. If I could only see Anny, the old hermit woman, who always cured everything with an herb. She always said, "Doctors may have studied, but they still don't know everything." I knew they nailed dead people into wooden boxes and opened up the ground to drop them in. At nights I dreamed my family stood around my grave, I watched my stepbrother Martin placing white daisies into an old rusty metal can as I saw him do each Sunday after church service when we visited the grave of his mother. I heard them pray for me and saw Mother replace the headstone with a small angel statue, the marking of a child's grave. That's when I screamed "No, no," waking myself up bathed in sweat. These dreams kept returning and frightening me.

But then one morning I woke up hearing birds outside an open window. I couldn't tell how much time had passed, I looked around. Was I dreaming or was I back in my old upstairs bedroom? I lay still, listening for familiar noises. It did not take long until I heard the squeaking of our water pump downstairs, the opening and closing of the old iron kitchen stove. All this assured me I was not dreaming, I was really home. What I could not remember was how I got into my own bed. I called for my mother as loud as I could. Minutes later she came in my room. I finally got the hugs and kisses I had been missing for such a long time. "Mom I am very, very hungry," I said and I wanted to smile, but all I could do was cry. Mother just held me in her arms and sobbed. She told me I had not eaten for some time and it was a good sign to be hungry. When she left the room to get me something to eat, I knew she would soon return. I was so glad to be home again, even this small bedroom I shared with my sister, which used to be part of the attic, without electricity and heat seemed now like heaven to me. Slowly I sipped the broth Mother had brought me and took a big bite of bread with our good home-churned butter. That was all I could manage. Feeling weak I lay back again, telling mom all the things that happened to me in the hospital. Mother told me about the letter she had received at Christmas. They believed I was dying and asked her to come. She could see me by climbing up a ladder outside the door looking through a small window. She refused to believe the skinny, pale looking girl was really me, until the nurse made me speak. Mother begged the doctor to discharge me. Since the hospital needed my bed and the doctor thought I was being more homesick than ill with scarlet fever I was returned home to either die or by a miracle to recover.

Mother had told me to rest and even though I was very tired, I could not sleep. Happy, I counted my blessings. Father had sent me a get-well letter with the promise to come home for my fourth birthday in April. His military-furlough days had been usually too short for me to get to know him very well. But I was sure at the end of the war our family could recover from all the pain of separation. I must have drifted off to sleep, because suddenly loud noises woke me up. Doors were banging, I heard my name being called and footsteps loud enough to collapse the staircase. But it was only my two stepbrothers Ernst and Martin and my sister Elisabeth returning home from school, fighting each other to be the first in my room. A few minutes later my sister stood in front of my bed, not knowing what to say. I could not remember what a sweet face she had, hair so blond and shiny and a smile of an angel. Behind her I saw Martin in his leather shorts with dark bruises on both knees, just as I remembered him. He took a seat at the foot of my bed, his dark curly hair hanging untamed over his forehead. And last was my brother Ernst, wearing his Hitler youth uniform that made him look all grown up, but his smile and freckled face told me he was still the boy I knew. He wore his glasses and looked extra smart. I promised myself never to make fun of him, like I done in the past. A few moments we silently observed each other. Those many months had turned us almost into strangers. Suddenly we all began to talk at once and laughter and happiness filled the upper room as never before. It was not until Mother called everyone handing out chores and telling them I needed rest.

I was alone again and cried but this time my tears were tears of joy. I knew now that love and being home was better than any medicine. Anny, the old hermit was right saying that doctors don't know everything. I wondered how she could be so smart without any schooling. Now instead of buried in a coffin six feet under, I was happy and safe tucked under my feather quilt upstairs in my bedroom. Later that evening, when Mother came to take care of me, she said it was only by the mercy and grace of our heavenly Father my life had been sustained. And I made her the promise, never to forget it.

WHEN THE CAT IS AWAY,
THE MICE WILL PLAY

School was closed today and my brothers were happy. Just as they were making plans how they could spend the day, Mother walked into the kitchen.

"Today is a good time for gathering firewood," she turned to the boy who made long faces. "You might want to go early, because it's supposed to rain in the afternoon." She looked nice, all dressed up for her dentist appointment. "And Elisabeth you make sure, Ilse-Dore eats every drop of her breakfast." Elisabeth nodded her head.

Because I was an extremely slow eater, Mother popped a second spoon next to my place. After she gave a few more instructions, she grabbed her raincoat, hat and purse and left. Martin kept watching her walk away through the window. I listened to the squeaking of the garden gate. When he reported she was out of sight, I pulled all those ugly lumps out of my apron pocket, and returned them to my cold milk soup. I hated those things. Why could she not one time make the soup without them. My dear sister allowed me to take it outside and dump the rest on Mother's compost pile. Then I covered up my crime with last night's potato peels I found lying everywhere.

It was not long, before the baker's kids came over. Guenther and Anni decided to play games and used most of the space on our kitchen table. That left Hiny and me the floor to play with our dolls. It was already after lunch, when we noticed it was raining. Suddenly it struck us like lightning, "the forgotten chore, the firewood." Now it was too late to go. Mother could come home any minute. The baker's kids left while we put up our toys and games and discussed what to do. Ernst turned pale and Martin cried, thinking about the stripes Mother handed out in good measure for disobedience.

"Maybe Mother won't remember by the time she gets home," I tried to cheer them up.

"Mother never forgets anything," Elisabeth replied. "But maybe we could do something about it."

There was not much time to talk things over. We had to act fast. Everyone was in on it to trick Mother. We ran into our wood shed and stuffed several sacks with pine cones and small sticks. Ernst, the oldest, turned into a regular artist, rearranging the wood pile and the pine cone box to make it look like nothing was missing. Martin and Elisabeth packed the sacks on the wagon, tying them down with a long rope. To make everything perfect, they pulled the wagon out of the wood shed until everything was wet, including their jackets, pants and boots. After they had pulled the wagon back into the shed, hung their wet garments up to dry and placed the boots next to the kitchen stove, they sat crossing their fingers while I sucked my thumb. Once more they discussed the matter, just to make sure they had not missed anything. And we waited.

It was not long, until Mother returned. She was wet, tired and hungry. She didn't ask anything until she saw the boots standing beside our stove. "Why didn't you go sooner this morning, as I told you?"

"The baker's kids came to play," Ernst said, using it for a perfect excuse. "We could not unload the sacks, because the ropes were too wet, but we pulled the wagon into the shed." Sighing relief he smiled at Mother.

It seemed to me, Mother got suspicious as soon as he mentioned the "baker's kids." She put her coat back on and went to the shed to see for herself how busy the boys had been. We all smiled at each other being proud of the right decision we had made. Soon this whole nightmare would be behind us. We all felt a close bond, like members of an underground organization, or at least of something important. But that feeling only lasted until Mother returned to the kitchen. There was some suspicion in her smile and her voice when she said, "You sure tried to do a perfect job."

"I know we should have gone sooner," Ernst apologized.

"Yes, you should. You might have even gotten away with your crime."

"But they did go, Mother," I ran up to her, convincing her. I rather lied than to see them punished.

"Yes, as far as the shed." Mother pushed me aside, grabbed Ernst who looked as white as a sheet, by his arm and pulled him to the window. "If you can show me some tire tracks on our muddy garden path, I might believe you."

Martin sat there crying. Elisabeth was pale and shaking, my face was red and my heart beating fast. We had overlooked one single thing, to make tracks on our long wet path in front and around the house. Father had mentioned one time that it was the minor details that gave away the crimes prisoners had committed, while they were investigated.

My parents and me.

Well, everyone was called one by one into the pump room to get the reward Mother handed out for lying, besides me. I already had received my share after I got up, even before I dressed, because I had again wet my bed. The doctor could not cure my bladder infection and the herb tea Mother brewed was not helping a lot. Maybe she thought her spankings would help to cure it. The children cried after Mother was finished disciplining them, but they were not the only ones hurt, I could tell it was also Mother's hands she had not spared.

That rainy afternoon had taught us all a very valuable lesson, never to disobey your parents, especially your mother and never deceive her. And in case we should have a notion to ever repeat it, to make sure we cover all our tracks.

THE HEIL HITLER AFFAIR

It was one week before Easter. I was up and around again. More often I caught myself watching the garden gate, hoping to see my father walking through unexpectedly. But the holiday passed and after it my birthday without any sign of him. Mother told me to be patient. Because so many soldiers had been killed in battle that needed to be replaced, my dad had to take on extra duty guarding trains, which transported military equipment and prisoners.

Finally Mother got ready to plant her vegetable garden like she did every year. She was nice to let me help by placing tiny seeds in the ground. She took me along gathering firewood and I had fun sitting in the wagon and when she walked to the forest ranger to get fresh milk, I could sit in my stroller because my legs were still too weak to carry me long distances. Sometimes I sat in front of our house, looking at the new fairy tale book my godmother had sent me for my birthday after she learned that the other one had to be left in the hospital since it could not be disinfected. This one was larger and contained a lot more pictures as well as fairy tales. Other times I watched the big kids getting ready for school in the morning or I would stand by the gate and wait for the Hitler youth to march by, holding their banner high. My big brother Ernst marched among them, singing of friendship and brotherhood, honor, loyalty unto death and love for our country. Mother didn't like some of the songs, especially the one that said "Today Germany is ours but tomorrow it will be the entire world." She just shook her head and said, "Pride comes before the fall."

Mom, and the rest of our town's little prayer group, put their trust in God's hands and not in the empty promises of our fanatic leader, Adolf Hitler. They said not everything about the man is bad. He had created jobs for people, giving child care help to sick mothers and child care money to large and low income families. He seemed to love children and made sure our country could be proud of its youth. "Children are the future of a country," he used to say in some of his speeches over the radio. He pulled families apart by making it mandatory different age groups met in his honor, like quilting, canning, and other things. The idea of a family as a unit was slowly being badly affected. Mother said I was born at a bad time right in the middle of the war. Now our country was fighting England and Russia. Some of our troops fought the British for colonies in Africa and the rest of the military were spread all over Europe, making sure, other countries kept their noses out of the war. No one seemed to know the real reason for what was happening. One evening, on one of our Fuehrer's important broadcasts he screamed, "We will fight until the last man!" Martin snickered and said, "By then I probably will be old and gray."

"And if you would be the only German man left alive, you would become our new Fuehrer," Elisabeth teased him. Mom turned off the radio, saying it was polluting our home.

The children had summer vacation. But for my brother Ernst, school time had ended—he was now fourteen. A baker in a small village nearby needed a clerk. Ernst, who had always shown an interest in baking, applied for this position and was accepted. One morning he packed his suitcase. There were tears in every eye, including his own, when he left.

"We will come to visit you sometimes," Mom told him, trying to cheer him up a bit to make his departure easier.

It was only a few days later that I woke up thinking about Ernst and how much I already missed him. Suddenly I noticed an unusual silence throughout the house. I woke my sister and we both listened, but the only thing we heard was Martin snoring in one of the boys' bunk beds, in the corner of our upstairs hallway. We woke him up, and all three of us sneaked down the stairs to investigate. There in the dim light of the morning, we noticed a long gray uniform coat hanging on our old coat rack. "It must be Father," Martin said while pointing at a pair of army boots next to it on the floor. We ran into the kitchen to greet him, but only Mother was sitting there, sorting out Father's luggage.

"You need to be quiet." She pointed toward the downstairs master bedroom. "He had a long journey and needs to rest." After breakfast, Martin and Elisabeth had to run an errand and I played outside, not to disturb Father. Ever since he had joined the military, everyone said he had changed. I could remember a time Father took our family mushroom seeking and berry picking or hiking in our large deep forest. Sometimes we had picnics and ballgames in the meadows. He used to do a lot of beautiful upholstery, working in the wood shed. When I was very little my memory of Father was only a pair of strong hairy arms holding me, a deep voice and a certain scent of tobacco. But the last few times on his furlough, he seldom came to church with us. He liked to spend his time in the trout lodge up the street. His need for attention had doubled, Mother said, and by putting other people's drinks on his tab he created a bill he could not cover. Each time he returned to his duty they were left for Mother to pay, and she worked them off by sewing for the trout lodge to keep our name spotless. I hoped this time it would be different. This time I was sure, his furlough would leave a good memory behind.

It was already noon when Father woke up. His mustache had turned sort of gray since I had seen him last time. In his bathrobe he looked so different than I remembered him. He hugged everyone, put me on his lap and asked me a lot of questions, which I politely answered. Later on, after he was dressed, he sat at the kitchen table answering all the questions Elisabeth and Martin had concerning our war. Mother was mending some of his clothes on her sewing machine, looking up smiling from time to time. While I played with my dolls, I was watching my dad from the distance, just listening and wishing that this portrait of family harmony would last forever. Sometimes I could feel him watching me playing and when I looked up, he was just smiling, not saying anything. And I was wondering if he felt the same way that I did once at the hospital. I was longing for home, for someone nice and gentle and wished for an end to all the bad things around me. After lunch, Father got all dressed up in his uniform. He needed to talk to someone at the trout lodge was his excuse, but he promised to return soon to spend the rest of the evening with us. Despite Mother's warning not to put too much trust in his promise, it made us all very happy and Elisabeth and Martin put their heads together to make plans for that special occasion. To Mother's big surprise, Father came home earlier than she had expected. He slammed the door shut, as if he would be angry. Mom had just returned from shopping and was still in the process to put up her groceries. "Is it true you did not greet our flag today?" He looked at Mom displeased and said it with an angry voice. Surprised, Mom paused, looking at him. "What do you mean by that?" she asked.

"You have been seen passing our town's flagpole without raising your hand and saying 'heil Hitler,'" explained Father.

We all knew just how much Mother hated to do that. She told me once, there was a time before I was born when people could greet each other any way they wanted, until our Nazi government made it mandatory to raise the right hand saying "heil Hitler," coming or leaving.

Mother was still staring at Dad while shaking her head. "What kind of idiot wastes time to spy on me, may I ask?" she asked with an ironic smirk on her face.

"If you must know, it was a most respected citizen," Father said, without revealing a name. "All I want to know is whether it is true." His voice had become extremely loud.

"I don't think I owe you an answer," Mom snapped. "I am not one of the prisoners you investigate here." Watching Father's face we all realized she had struck a delicate nerve. "Well I will tell you what happened, so you won't believe I am guilty of a crime," she continued. "Today, as I passed the flagpole the guard usually standing there was absent. I had both hands full of shopping bags and didn't find it necessary to say 'heil Hitler' to a piece of fabric. I hope no one expects me to speak to an object that neither can hear nor speak. I just don't feel like greeting a rag in the wind."

"What did you just call our flag?" screamed Father, his face turning as red as a lobster. And I was wondering, whether had it not been for the presence of us children, if he would have struck her since he jerked out of his chair, made one step toward her with his hand raised, but suddenly turned as if he remembered us watching. Mother just stood there, tall and unafraid like an iron statue one would not dare to hurt, just looking at him.

"How can you dishonor our flag, calling it a rag in the wind?" Father kept screaming. "It is the flag I fight under and millions of soldiers died for. You disrespect our fatherland and our Fuehrer. I better not do anything, I might later regret." He grabbed his uniform jacket and left the house, slamming our front door so hard I thought the roof might cave in. Martin tried to run after him, but Mother held him back.

"Never mind boy," she said. "He just found a good excuse to spend another night out to make more bills for me to pay. Besides, I don't understand what is so good about a leader who demands from us that we should hate our Jewish neighbors and friends. I have a problem with honoring a flag that is used to arrest and puts innocent people into prison. Maybe Father has a war out there, but we at home are fighting our own war with conscience. Maybe our government believes it has us blindfolded. Once in a while we see their unrighteousness." Mother spoke with haste, her voice shaking. "Last year," she turned to me, "when you were still in the hospital and the children in school, hundreds of Jews were driven through our town like a herd of cattle toward Poland. There were old people and a lot of children who could hardly walk anymore. Some of them were younger than you." She took off her glasses to wipe away her tears.

It turned out to be a sad evening in our house. All the things we had planned to do with Father had to be postponed. Martin stood at the window, staring into the darkness. Elisabeth kept flipping the pages of one of her school books and I sat on the little footstool in front of the kitchen stove. There was a war inside of it that only I was aware of. I looked through the little glass door, watching the fire burn until I saw houses burn, people running and whole cities being on fire. But it all stopped when Mother said it was time for bed.

Mother came upstairs to pray with us. As a goodnight snack she gave us one of our beautiful, large winter apples. My sister ate hers a lot faster than I did and complained afterwards of all the noise I made eating, until I let her have the rest of mine. Suddenly we heard our bedroom door squeak. A dark shadow crept in. In front of my sister's bed it stood still. "Do you know, Mom could be arrested for what she has said about our flag?" It was only Martin whispering

Left: Charlotte & Ernst. Right: Anna & Martin.
Middle: My parents and my sister Elisabeth.

in the dark of the room. "How can she be arrested? Nobody but us heard what she said," Elisabeth answered.

Well, our wonderful dream spending a weekend with Father ended in the morning when we found out he had left early without telling us goodbye. Maybe it was true that people changed in the military. All the good feelings of love and compassion were being slowly replaced with hate and heroism and turned into fanatics. Maybe it was wrong to blame Father only.

THE VISIT

"Time heals all wounds" they say. Life went back to normal and the memory of the terrible argument between my parents slowly faded in my mind.

"Take a look, little one, something must be up," said Mom while stirring her applesauce to keep it from burning. Our neighbor's dog and the squeaking of the gate were a duet, followed usually by a visitor. I climbed up on the window bench to take a look. A tall man in uniform came walking toward the house.

"It's a man, Mom!" I called out to her. Quickly she set the pot aside and came to see for herself.

"It's our mayor," she said nervously. "Last time he came, you were still in the hospital. He brought a telegram that informed us Anna's husband had been killed on the Russian front."

This time it had to be about dad, who didn't say goodbye to us, I thought. We only had two men in the war, my oldest stepsister Anna's husband who froze to death in the mountains of Russia and my father. I watched Mother folding her hands beneath her kitchen apron making a silent prayer. She went to open the door for our visitor who greeted us with a loud "heil Hitler" as he entered.

"Has anything happened to my...?"

"No, no," he said calmly before she could finish her sentence, noticing how worried she was. "I came on a totally different matter." He took the seat Mother offered him and laid his hat on the table, while he pointed at a chair close by. "You might want to sit down before I bring you this news," he said politely, and Mother, hiding her hands beneath her apron again, followed his advice. For a few

21

seconds he looked Mom straight in the face, after that he looked down at his hands as if he had forgotten what he came to say or what he didn't really want to say. "I don't know how to say this to you..." He still kept looking at his hands. "There was a report made against you that states you dishonored our flag including our fatherland." Mother stared at him with disbelief. "Do you remember saying our flag is nothing but a rag in the wind?" Intensely gazing at her, he was waiting for an answer. Mother hesitated as if she needed time digesting such news. The mayor waited quietly. He looked at me and smiled. "I only know you as a loyal citizen, an excellent mother and as a faithful wife. Maybe there was a misunderstanding. But I need to know what exactly has happened, before this report gets into the hands of our Gestapo, who will arrest you." He urged Mother to speak.

Suddenly Mom had this helpless look on her face and I could tell she was close to tears. But soon she gained control and told our mayor everything about that night before Father left.

"Your husband made excellent use of his training investigating prisoners and trapped you into making a statement, which later can be held against you," he said, after he had listened quietly. "Now we need to come up with something we can use for defense. I would hate to see you being arrested and knowing your husband longer than you..." He suddenly stopped talking, looking around until his eyes rested upon the picture of our Fuehrer that hung in one corner of our kitchen. "At least it shows you honor our leader," he said satisfied.

Suddenly Mom came up with the idea to show him her little notebook containing most of her poems. "Perhaps you can find something in here." She handed it to him.

He opened it and looked long and carefully through the handwritten pages. Mom called her poetic talent a gift from God. Sometimes she made me run into the kitchen to fetch her book and a pencil. I watched her writing her poem quickly, line after line. When she was finished, she read it to me, everything rhymed perfectly. When I asked her how she did it, she smiled and said, "It's like flowing water. As the Lord turns it on, the water flows, and when it's finished, He turns it off."

The mayor seemed to be finished with Mom's book. "I love your poems and I believe I have found one or two I would like to use, of course with your permission." He pulled some paper from his pocket, asked Mom for a pen and copied several pages. "These poems are a window to your soul," he said, smiling at her. "I believe I just now begin to know and respect you." With these words he returned the little book to Mom, who thanked him.

"I don't think I have to warn you to be more careful choosing your words next time your husband is at home. I've known him longer and better than you. Whenever you have a discussion with him, keep this report in mind. Will you promise me that?" He got up,

My father home on furlough.

giving Mom an extra warm smile. He walked to the door and turned around, facing us once more. His smile had left his face as he raised his right arm and with a loud "heil Hitler," clicked the heels of his boots together. He turned around again and left, not waiting for her to respond.

She closed the door, took me by my hand and sank on her knees, thanking God for His help. She cried for some time and I just stood there not knowing what to do. Somehow I wanted to wish something bad for my dad or for anyone that tried to hurt my mother.

"There are still good people," she said after she stopped crying, "and some of them even wear a Nazi uniform like our mayor. Thank God not everyone is a Nazi by heart."

I didn't see my dad again until after the war was over. The memory he had left behind made a deep, and permanent scar in my heart.

THE BIG LIE

It was Sunday morning and time to get ready for church. Mother helped me to put on my best dress.

"You are either growing too fast, or your dress is shrinking," she said, looking at my legs.

"I want to be as tall as you Mom, so I can reach up to God." Smiling I looked at her, that tall giant from the Baltic coast, full of energy and straight as a candlestick.

She returned my smile. "Yes, maybe I am a few inches closer to God than some people around here, but it is not the height that reaches the Lord, but the heart and prayer. Promise me you'll listen to your brother and sister today, since they have been doing such an excellent job taking you along to church. If she only knew what was really happening. I got dropped off each Sunday, while the kids went to the picture show. They showed movies about our German soldiers fighting the war and Martin said the school had made it mandatory to watch them. It all began when Mother took on her Sunday morning job helping Mrs. Mueller with her crippled son.

It was time to leave. "Watch over your sister," Mom lectured my siblings. "Don't walk too fast, don't soil your good Sunday clothes and listen good, so you can tell me later what the pastor preached today." I had the feeling nobody was really listening and in a hurry to get out of Mother's sight. As usual she stood at the door, watching us leave. And as most of the time, I was the only one turning around at the gate, waving and smiling. If she only knew I felt more like crying, being put in the position to keep my sister and brother out of trouble. At church, Martin pushed me in one of the empty pews right in front of the altar. "Listen to what the pastor preaches so you can tell us about it. We'll wait for you again outside the door like we always do after the service."

"Yes," I whispered, bravely trying to hide my tears and the sudden powerful impulse to run home to Mother, confiding in her and sobbing into her apron. But hopefully Mother would never find out, because she raised us with the Scriptures in mind, especially the verse, "children obey your parents." And in case the commandment "you shall not lie," had slipped our minds, she made sure we remembered it, because "who-so-ever loves his children does not spare the rod" was one of her favored verses. She just never had to use a rod, since her hands were as hard as steel and once one felt them, one wanted to obey for the rest of one's life. "Just remember what kind of trouble Mom could cause for us complaining to those Nazi teachers and remember what you promised us," I could still hear my sister telling me.

The organ began to play and the pastor entered. I looked at that man of God standing there tall in his black robe, having his eyes focused upon me again. Each time I felt like melting into the ground. Just like last Sunday he raised his bushy eyebrows as if he wanted to say, "Child, why are you here all alone?" It made me move a few inches deeper into the bench, but I still could not manage to escape his sight. Suddenly a sunbeam crossed the pew. Its bright light made me close my eyes. I sat there feeling its warmth upon my face and I started dreaming of a time I used to sit like that leaning against my mother's warm body with my eyes closed just as now. Our entire family would sit together, even Dad sometimes when he was home on furlough. They said I was their little "nest egg" and had to sit right between Mom and Dad. But now I wondered if I was only being used as a social divider between them. Maybe it all had started with the argument I accidentally overheard one day.

I had been sent outside to play in our sandbox. I had forgotten one of my dolls and went back inside to get her. The bedroom door was cracked, so I could hear them talk. Father was telling Mother about the highway the prisoners had to build through the Alpine mountains. Money to feed the large number of prisoners had been used for the war effort and all were starved, weak and sick. After the project was completed, they all had to line up behind each other on the street they had been building. While a large street roller was used to crush their bodies into the asphalt, German soldiers lined up on both sides to shoot everyone that tried to escape. Father had stopped talking. First was silence. Then Mother sobbed and screamed, "Henry how could you?" Father tried to explain. "In the army you follow orders, I couldn't help them." Again I heard Mother cry out, "Don't you touch me Henry." That's when I crept backwards out of the house, wishing I had never been listening to my parents' conversation. To seek some comfort, I sat in the sandbox hugging my doll and sucking my favorite thumb. "That's the reason why your thumb is so short, look at it," I remember Ernst telling me, just before he left to work in the bakery. I pulled it out of my mouth and matched it against my other thumb and smiled. I swore next time I saw Ernst, I would show him. But as I studied it a little closer I had to admit, it seemed just a little bit wider, however, that was only for me to know.

Suddenly the organ played the last hymn. I had completely forgotten to listen to the pastor. I guessed I had to do what I had done up until now and that was to come up with another Bible story. While I walked toward the exit I tried to remember one I had not yet used. I had used Jonah and the whale, Joseph in bondage, David and Goliath and suddenly my mind went blank. My brother and sister were waiting for me. Martin asked what subject our preacher had used today. I felt more like crying than talking. I looked at the two large angel statues guarding the gate to the cemetery. There was my story for today. "Today he spoke of the glory of God and the angels appearing in Bethlehem saying: 'Fear not...'" That was the end of my speech, because Martin highly upset jerked my arm.

"That can't be true," he said. "Nobody tells a Christmas story in the middle of the summer." Helpless I looked at my sister, and suddenly had the feeling she knew all along I was making things up, only to please everyone. "Let go of her," she said. "So, maybe she is not telling the truth but we do the same to Mother. Besides, that 'fear not' might just fit into these times because everyone is scared of the war." Of course Martin didn't agree right away, but all the way home, we could not come up with anything better.

Mother had prepared a good lunch and was waiting for us. Only this time my dear brother used the outhouse for the longest time. Maybe he hoped the investigation about church ceremony would be over by the time he returned. But for some strange reason Mother never asked us anything about it that Sunday.

THE TRUTH REVEALED

Elisabeth woke me to help her zip up the back of her dress. "I wish I could go to school," I said, watching her slip into her shoes. "It's not that much fun anymore since we have Miss Bengner. All she likes to do is talk about politics, the war and everything." She brushed her shiny, wavy hair to braid it back into pigtails. "You are better off staying home with Mother."

I thought about it. Maybe she was right. But what about all that lying we had managed so well each Sunday? What about next and the following weekends? "Wouldn't it be better if we told Mother the truth?" I suggested, pulling the quilt up to my nose.

She whipped around as if she was stung by a bee. "Don't you ever again let that thought cross your mind," she whispered as though someone was listening. "You have no idea what the outcome could be." Perhaps Elisabeth was right, maybe I should put all unpleasant thoughts out of my mind, at least until next Sunday. I turned around to sleep a little longer, but it was too late. Mother just walked in to help me dress.

After breakfast I was watching Mother putting new sheets on our beds, when suddenly we heard someone knocking at the front door. Mom rushed downstairs and I was standing in the middle of the staircase when I heard her say, "What an honor" as she had opened the door. And there in the morning sunlight with the sweetest smile on her face, stood our pastor's wife. I just tried to turn around to run back upstairs, when I heard her say, "Is that your youngest daughter?"

"Yes," replied Mother. She turned to me. "Come and say hello." It was too late to hide. I grabbed for the banister, feeling a certain weakness in my knees. "I have been admiring her each Sunday, sitting in that large pew all alone," continued our lovely visitor.

"Ilse-Dore, come down at once." Mother looked at me, and it seemed as if her eyes were growing behind her glasses. I approached her as cautiously as possible knowing I now was walking into hell's fire. In the meantime Mother had turned to our visitor. "But I always send her in the company of her older brother and sister."

"You don't know, your little girl gets dropped off and picked up after church service?" Confused and surprised the pastor's wife looked at me, and in Mother's eyes began to burn an angry fire.

"Is it true?" asked Mother, turning to me, raising her voice. I took one more look at the lady standing there like an angel sent from heaven to reveal the truth. I surely couldn't accuse her of lying. Just nodding I hung my head low. But Mother was not satisfied. She would make me talk. I felt her iron hand reaching under my chin, pulling it higher and higher, until I no longer could prevent looking into her angry eyes. I finally stood on my toes to keep my neck from stretching and hurting. "Yes," I squeezed out. That was exactly what she wanted to hear. Immediately she let go of me. "You stay close by, you hear?" she said satisfied.

Our visitor joined Mother in the kitchen to discuss this matter of betrayal. I sat in the corner of the bottom step of the staircase and cried, knowing what was ahead. Surely she would have mercy on me, if she heard about the new rule the school had and how we all were afraid to tell her. But I found out how wrong I was, as soon as our smiling visitor had left. "I will teach you not to lie," she said and before I could speak she held me over her knee and spanked me until my lower backside felt like fire. Then she sent me upstairs to my bedroom, where I fell on my bed crying into my pillow, using it for a sound barrier until I finally fell asleep.

I woke up, hearing Elisabeth and Martin coming home from school. I rushed to the door to warn them, but found it locked. I placed my ear close to the keyhole to listen. Mother called them separately into the kitchen. All I could hear was loud voices, followed by spanking and crying. Finally Mom came upstairs to unlock the door and tell me to come down for lunch. My siblings looked at me with their tearstained eyes as though I was Judas coming for the last supper. They both must have believed I betrayed them and were just waiting for Mom to leave the house to hit or push me for telling on them. There was a long silence at the table. All one could hear was the clicking of the silverware and the swallowing of the food. Each time Mother passed the food around, I could tell her hands were hurting her.

"I want to know, why you all have been deceiving me like this?" she broke the silence.

Martin finally had the courage to tell her about the new rule, the teacher and how afraid we had been that she might confront the teacher and get herself in trouble with the Third Reich. Mother seemed shocked. "I had no idea... Why didn't you tell me this before I spanked you?"

Mother, Elisabeth and I.

"You never give us a chance. Sometimes if we open our mouth to defend ourselves, you spank us even harder," Elisabeth explained and the rest of us nodded.

Mother stared at us. We knew she was sorry, but it was too late now. "Let's just hope that God soon puts an end to Nazi teachers ruling our schools," she said and it almost sounded like a prayer. "It was our pastor's wife who paid us a visit and brought light into this darkness, not your little sister telling on you." Maybe Mom had sensed what they were thinking by the way they looked at me. Now I was free of that Judas sign hanging around my neck and Martin and Elisabeth smiled at me again.

THE CONFRONTATION

Ernst said once, "Mom is like a drop of water trying to flow against the stream." She had decided to talk to Miss Bengner. And when she made up her mind about something, there was no way stopping her. "Be careful, Mom, you don't know our teacher. She has the entire Third Reich backing her up, these Nazis have power you do not have." Martin pleaded with her, while she stuffed an apple and sandwich into his backpack. Then she followed him and my sister to the door to see them off to school.

"Don't worry, Martin," I heard her say. "I may not be able to change anything, but at least I will feel better knowing I tried to do something about that ungodly force."

As every morning, I pulled a chair up to the window to watch the kids waiting at the gate until they could join the rest of the school children who came from the upper part of the village. I kept dreaming about the day I would be a school girl, too, and no longer have to listen to "Why don't you go and suck your little thumb," "This is not for baby ears," "You can't run fast enough," or "First you need to grow up." It certainly was not my fault I was born so much later than my siblings, but somehow I had to take the blame for it.

After Mother completed her morning chores and asked the Lord for His blessings, we were on our way to see the teacher who had caused us so much heartache. On the way to school we had to pass the Liebig house, the place we spent our Sunday afternoons in prayer meetings. Mr. Liebig was chopping firewood in his yard.

"I could feel you were coming," he said, putting down his ax. "I sense the little one as well." He bent down to touch my face. I

looked up into his foggy gray eyes that could not see me, because old
Mr. Liebig had been blind since birth.

"I find it amazing how you prepare your firewood year after
year," Mother said, shaking her head.

"You know all things are possible with the Lord," he answered
and a glorious smile was covering his face. Mother told me once he
had an "inward eye" God gave him to see with. We could only see
what was on the outside of a person, but Mr. Liebig could see what
was on the inside of one, just by shaking that person's hand. I had
an utmost respect for that tall, skinny man with those large calloused
hands and that long gray beard. And while Mother stayed a few minutes to visit, I spent some time out back in the stable watching the
young little rabbits play. Finally Mother called me. It was time to go.
Mrs. Liebig watched us from the open window.

"Don't be discouraged, God is still in command," she called.
Mom just waved at her and then we crossed the road and entered the
schoolyard.

The children were out on recess, it looked as if we had chosen just the right time. We walked through a long hallway. Mother
stopped in front of a door that was decorated with the sign of the
Third Reich and knocked. A loud voice asked us to enter.

"Heil Hitler," said a lady sitting behind a huge desk before
she introduced herself as Miss Bengner. By no means did this woman look as I had pictured her, mean and ugly. She had the friendli-
est smile, she wore a beautiful sparkling broach on her white lace
collar, and wore her hair in braids around her head. She offered us
to sit at the two chairs across from her desk. Mother and I took a
seat.

"I am Martin's mother," Mom introduced herself, "and I won't
take up much of your time." She looked at that big stack of papers
piled up on top of the desk.

The teacher smiled at us. "I am sure you came to discuss his
great talent in art?" she asked.

"I came to solve the situation about Sunday's church service," Mother said quietly.

Immediately Miss Bengner took off her glasses and laid them on her desk. She crossed her arms, leaned forward and stared at Mother. "Keep talking, I must say I admire your courage," she said with a funny smirk on her face.

"See, I look at it this way," Mother tried to explain. "Six days you may tell my children what to do, but on Sunday I am in command, I am their mother. I have the right to tell them to go to church."

"I am not the one to blame, I did not put a stop to church visits," the teacher explained. She was no longer smiling. "It is the rule of our Third Reich that children have to attend these educational movies. Your children are obeying and I would advise you to do the same," she said, with a tone of authority in her voice. "As I recall," she continued, "aren't you the woman who called our flag 'a rag in the wind?'" She smiled sarcastically.

"Look here," Mother said, totally ignoring her last remark, "I am not here to disobey any law. All I ask is, to have the movie time changed, so my children can go to church on Sunday morning. Besides, I believe to obey God should be first in everyone's life."

Miss Bengner got up from her chair. Like a statue she stood suddenly in front of us looking down with her eyebrows raised. "You have no right to tell our government to make changes in rules and regulations. And if you open your mouth only one more time, I will see to it personally that you will be arrested this time."

Mother who had just opened her mouth was unable to form any words. Silently she got up and took my hand and I could tell she was shaking as we walked toward the door.

"Heil Hitler!" screamed Miss Bengner's ugly voice behind us. Mother just raised her hand without saying a word.

"Excuse me please, did you forget to say something?" shouted the teacher behind us. "Heil Hitler," said Mother just as we left the room. On our way home Mother had to stop several times to clean her glasses and blow her nose.

"Are you crying, Mother?" I asked. "Just a little," she replied. "I do honor our fatherland, even if they don't think so. I just don't like it when words are being forced on us, like saying 'Heil Hitler.' Words have power, they can make someone very happy or very sad or put one behind bars or even get one killed. God's word has power. He created the entire world just with words." She looked down to me, smiled and stroked my hair. "You are so young now, but some-day you will understand all of that."

"You think I will have a nice teacher when I go to school?" I asked, hoping not to get an old witch like Miss Bengner.

"With God all things are possible," Mom replied, looking back to the Liebig residence, and I thought about all that firewood in the garden that Mr. Liebig had chopped with his blind eyes.

Mother and I.

TYPHOID FEVER

With summer's end Mother kept busy canning vegetables, preserving fruits and dehydrating mushrooms and berries of all sorts. I helped string apple slices to be hung up for drying. Because Hiny's mother had found a part-time job, he had become my now almost every day playmate. Hiny had a head full of untamable blond curls, which Mother referred to as "sheep's wool." He was a little younger than I and because he had short legs, he dragged our footstool to the outhouse to climb up to the high wooden throne. His appetite had no limits—he loved to stuff his little cheeks anytime with anything edible. Like a little hamster sent from heaven at breakfast, he took care of all those ugly flour lumps I handed him under the table when Mom was too busy to watch us. Even after I finished eating my milk soup, he still held his little hands open for more. He was a big help each time we played in our sandbox because he got rid of all the ugly worms and bugs for me that I was afraid to touch.

One day Mother became very ill. Typhoid had spread in our village and claimed some lives. Mother was hospitalized and my oldest stepsister Charlotte came home to replace her until she got well. Our doctor discovered my immunity to typhoid and suggested to isolate me, because carrying germs made me a danger to everyone around. Once again I had to endure several months of hospitalization being in good health laying among the sick and dying. I was allowed to be in Mom's room she shared with two more ladies. Because many nurses had been sent to the battlefield, there was a shortage and the room smelled so bad. A lot of times it made me feel too sick to eat. Mom tried to keep me entertained but was so weak she made it only through part of a fairy tale. The rest of the story I had to dream up myself. One morning the nurse told me to turn the other way and stay in this position. After she had left the room, I got suspicious and turned. I saw a mountain of pink flesh with an ugly sore on it totally uncovered in the bed across the aisle. A lamp had been placed in a chair next to it to lighten up this embarrassing situation. Everyone, including Mom, was deep asleep. Being sure I was of help to the poor lady, I turned off the lamp and covered up the sore with her sheet. It made the nurse very angry at me, and for interfering with the healing of a bed sore I no longer could stay in Mom's room.

The next day I was transferred to a large room full of empty beds. I felt punished waking up each morning in the company of bed bugs. They were hiding deep inside the mattress and attacked me at night when it was dark. Each time the night nurse put me on the bedpan, my sheet was covered with bed ticks, looking like moving polka dots. Finally a man came and treated the bed frames with a bad smelling solution. He said soldiers had caused these bed ticks to spread in the hospital. The whole room smelled so bad, I spent most of my time under my cover crying and calling for my mother who could not hear me. During sleep I scratched open some of those countless tick bites. After the nurse found enough blood on my sheet, I was finally freed from this prison and sent to another large room full of typhoid sick children. For the first time I could breathe again without crawling under the blanket. But soon I found out I had another problem. It was the famous "bucket" being used by everyone who was able to walk. They had put it in the corner right behind my bed. Several times a day someone came to empty it, spray it with Lysol and cover it with a bent lid that would not stay on. Some of these children cried out in pain and called for their mothers. I was so glad I was immune to this disease. A girl named Helga, who occupied a bed nearby, began to talk to me each time she came to use the bucket. Just like me, she was not ill and we both felt happy to have found someone to talk to.

Children left and new ones were admitted. Twin boys, who were placed in beds on the other side of the room, seemed to be as healthy as Helga and I. We watched them going around and snatch the food from the trays of some of the sick children. By night they sneaked around in the moonlight with sheets pooled over their heads to scare the sick children. Helga, who was a few years older than I, reported it to the nurses. We waited, but nothing happened. Finally Helga came up with a plan that sounded like a perfect solution. Just once we wanted to hear the twins scream. And one night it happened. While the two boys left to get some sheets from the linen closet in the hallway, Helga came to get the bucket. In the moonlight I watched her pouring some of its contents between the sheets of the twin boys' beds. We snickered as she returned the bucket. She went to her bed, covered up and waited. The boys returned, performing their nightmare dressed as ghosts creeping from bed to bed, making strange noises to scare the children. Finally the ugly entertainment was over. I held my breath watching them both jump into their beds at the same time. And then we heard what we had so long been waiting for. Two screams, so long and loud the night nurse came running and turned on the light. Of course Helga and I had no idea what had just happened. We rubbed our eyes as if we had been sleeping. "Those poor boys," we said, "who would do such a terrible thing." But I was sure after everything was cleaned up and the lights turned out, that Helga smiled herself to sleep just like I did. The next day the twins asked around to find the guilty person. But nobody talked. From that night on the children could sleep again in peace and I was proud of Helga and her courage.

Several months passed and with them another Christmas. The epidemic was finally over. We received a disinfecting bath and were discharged. Like risen from the dead, on the hand of my dear Mother, I stood outside that gray sandstone building remembering all the time I had spent with scarlet fever behind those large windows. It had robbed me of two Christmas seasons and I hoped

I would never have to come back again. Filling up my lungs with plenty of fresh air, I felt like jumping and running and most of all happy to go home.

"The best and most beautiful things in the world cannot be seen or even touched. They must be felt within the heart."
HELEN KELLER

VACATION

As happy as I was to be home again, as sad I felt to find out Charlotte had left. The snow was melting and the first snow bells began to bloom. One weekend we took a long walk through a large and dark forest to visit with Ernst. Another time we hiked to the forest ranger estate, where Mother used to live as a house seamstress, before she married. Easter came and passed and for my fifth birthday the mailman brought us a package from Father and a letter from Mom's sister Lena. Because she worked as a secretary for a post office, she knew more about the war than most people. In her letter she begged Mother to come home and see the Baltic once more before the destruction of Germany. Since I was the youngest and still out of school, I was allowed to join Mom on her trip.

It was a long train ride through Poland. Mother's home was at the Baltic coast, East Prussia, a small section of Germany located between Poland and Russia. My grandparents had died long before I was born, but my three aunts still lived together in a large house next to the canal. Ships came here from all over the world delivering goods to be stored in large warehouses. Anywhere we wanted to go, we had to cross the canal with a small ferryboat. Walking along the majestic seashore, I now could understand Mom being so homesick. I remembered how she use to turn on the running water at our kitchen sink or each time we went hiking in the forest past the waterfall, just so she could hear running water to remember the sea. I loved to feel the white, warm beach sand between my toes and collect pretty seashells. Sometimes I searched for honey-colored amber pieces in green slimy piles of washed ashore seaweeds. Bright yellow Ginster were blooming along the sand dunes and behind it all I could see gigantic pines standing along the back of the beach to hold off the icy winds of the sea during the winter. During cloudbursts or a passing thunderstorm we could seek shelter in one of the beautiful elevated restaurants that were built along the shore and while waiting for the rain to cease, could enjoy some refreshments. One morning I saw my first U-boat. Just like a large fish slowly rising out of the water, it came up in the far distance. The crew looked like small toy people, lining up on deck saluting toward the shore.

My three aunts gave me so much attention that sometimes I felt like I had four mothers instead of one. I wished I could have canned all those many hugs and kisses I received, like Mom and her summer harvest to enjoy them later on rainy days of my life. It was a summer with sun, water, sand and blueberry picking. Every day was filled with new excitement until one night ended it all. It was the first air raid. The Russians had begun to bomb the harbor. Mother helped me to slip into my coat and shoes, grabbed my backpack and rushed me downstairs to safety, while she went back upstairs to pack our suitcases. I sat there in the cold, dark and damp cellar all alone on a bench next to a small flickering candle shaking with fear, hoping and praying the draft wouldn't put out the flame. Over and over I could hear the planes coming down low and lower until I thought they touched the tip of the house. Each time a bomb exploded, the whole ground shook and everything inside the cellar vibrated. Finally Mother and her sisters came carrying a bunch of suitcases. We waited and waited until finally another siren called off the air raid.

The next morning, it was still dark when Mother dressed me and said it was getting too dangerous to stay any longer. When it was time to leave, all my aunts cried and hugged us, as if we would never see each other again. We left with the first train. It was at the border changing trains, when we noticed everyone around us spoke Polish. Because our Nazi Germany was causing problems in Poland, people no longer liked us.

"It is best for you to pretend you can't speak," Mother whispered. "It seems we are the only Germans on board." When someone asked Mother a question, she answered in Polish. I knew she had grown up among Polish and Russian-speaking people. Some of the passengers put their heads together and whispered and I was wondering if it was about us. We were dressed different and the way some looked at us gave me a scary feeling. I was glad when our train stopped in a large city. Mother took me outside to buy something to drink. On the way we passed a German officer reading his newspaper. While Mother paid for the drink, he smiled at me, asking for my name and how old I was. After I politely answered, he began to speak to Mother. When he found out what train we were on, he seemed to be concerned for our safety. He asked us to wait until he could make different travel arrangements for us. A few minutes later he returned, taking us to another train and sent for our luggage. This one was guarded by German soldiers. We had a whole compartment to ourselves. The maroon upholstered seats were soft and almost too nice to sit on. It was not just clean, but even smelled good. Mother and the officer were both deep in a conversation about their homeland. He had the same Baltic accent as Mom did. I leaned out of the window, watching all the different passengers. An announcement came over the speaker that our train was ready to leave. The officer got up, grabbed his coat and smiled at me. "Take good care of your dear Mother," he said, pulling softly on one of my braids. I watched him take Mother's hand into his. He held it and finally cupped it with his other hand as if he was afraid she would pull it back. There was an adoring expression in his face. I looked at Mom. I didn't notice anything different about her. She just stood there in front of him with her hand still captured in his, tall and strong and pretty, a soft blue silk scarf wrapped around her hat matching her eyes, and grandmother's amber broach holding the lace collar pinned to her dark-brown woolen dress.

"He sure likes you very much, Mom," I said after he had left. I watched him walk away outside the train. Once he turned and waved at me, I waved back.

"What makes you think that?" asked Mother, her cheeks all red.

"Oh, I just know," I replied, keeping my thoughts a secret.

"Maybe he is missing his mother, or his wife, someone he loves," she explained, closing the window while looking out. But he was no longer in sight. "Probably each time Father sees a blond little pigtailed girl, he looks at her, thinking of you," she said.

"What about you, does he not miss you, too?" I wondered.

"Perhaps a little." Her voice was almost a whisper. Suddenly a loud whistle interrupted our conversation. A small jerk told us the train had begun to move. A German soldier opened the door and asked us if we needed anything. Mother assured him we were fine. He smiled politely and left. I leaned my tired head against the soft cushion and thought about how nice the officer had cared for us and how proud his little girl could be of her father, if he had one.

It's me watering flowers!

SWAMP LIGHTS

It was late in the afternoon. Martin and Guenther worked on a secret project, little Hiny was sick and their sister Anni had no one to play with because Elisabeth was spending some time in Berlin with our cousin. "You want to watch ghost lights?" Anni asked me standing at the gate.

"Well, ok, but you know my mom, I have to be back home before dark," I replied.

"Don't worry there is plenty of daylight left. Maybe I should take my grandfather's cane along," she suggested.

"Let's just go and forget the cane," I said. Having been warned by my sister not to completely trust her and remembering how merciless she had beaten that frog to death last year, gave me the shivers. "Not that I am afraid," she laughed and paused, "I just thought a stick would come handy in case we had to defend ourselves."

"I'm not scared," I replied, and grabbed my sweater. Taking a shortcut, we crossed the street, passed by Sempert's farm and from there followed a narrow hiking trail. We crossed a brook and ran across a large meadow. At the end we climbed a steep hill and had reached the end of our journey. Almost out of breath we fell into the grass, resting and looking down the other side of the hill. And there it was, the place people began to whisper each time they mentioned it, as if they had to hide a deep dark secret, "Judgment meadow." Deep in the valley, it reached from the foot of the hill all the way to the beginning of the dark green pine forest. Tonight the fog hovered ghostly over the grass. On warm and humid summer nights blue lights had been sighted performing a ghostly dance.

Villagers believed these were the restless souls of lost people, being held captive until judgment day. Side by side Anni and I laid in the tall grass, looking downhill, watching and waiting for the sun to go down and the appearing of the lights. "Are you scared?" Anni asked me.

"No not yet," I replied, thinking of the many times I had accompanied my mother picking berries and finding mushrooms or gathering pine cones in the dark forest.

"Just think, if one would fall downhill and end up in the middle of a bunch of ghost lights," Anni said suddenly. She was a few years older, taller and stronger than me and the way she looked at me, gave me a strange feeling. Not being sure if she just wanted to scare me or push me downhill, caused me to move a little away from her.

"Actually I have already been down there walking across the meadow," I informed her.

"You did what?" Anni stuttered in disbelief, forgetting to close her mouth.

I nodded my head. "Together with my mother, not long ago," I assured her.

"What was it like? Did someone grab or follow you?"

I laughed. "Of course not," I said. "I just picked some of that special white wool grass that only seems to grow down there, besides, it was a very warm and sunny afternoon," I explained.

"Heavens, cursed flowers," she said being shocked. "You did not really take them home with you."

"Why shouldn't I, I still have them. Mother said they will last forever, because they don't need any water, but they also don't have any fragrance."

"Because they are dead," Anni said. "Dead flowers belong to the dead. Your mother should have never let you pick them."

"My mother is not superstitious. There is no such thing as lost souls dancing in a meadow," I replied. "She says what some people sighted were nothing but swamp lights, because they have swamps where she was born. And the day we walked across the meadow the ground was extremely moist and hot."

"That's it," Anni whispered. "Lost souls, dead flowers and hell's fire beneath the ground. How come your mother does not believe the way we do? Does she think she is smarter than we are?"

"I don't think my mother tries to be smarter than anybody here. She comes from the Baltic coast and knows different things," I tried to explain.

"That's exactly it." Anni seemed to have found an answer. "Some believe your mother thinks she is royalty and better than all of us. That's why she walks so straight like a queen or candlestick. I also heard she does not like to say 'heil Hitler' and she can't get along with your father and she is a bad stepmother to his children and on Sunday she joins a stupid prayer group. That makes her a real religious fanatic." Totally shocked I stared at Anni. I could hardly follow her ugly accusations as fast as they poured out of her mean mouth. Close to tears, I thought of something to say to defend my mother.

Suddenly there was a strange noise nearby. We looked down into the valley but nothing had changed. Only the sun had set and the daylight was fading fast. Anni's eyes expressed sudden fear. Another sound followed, coming from the same direction as the first. It almost sounded as if someone was calling. Anni suddenly screamed in fear, jumped to her feet and took off running, leaving me behind. I tried to follow her, but remembering my sweater was still in the grass I returned to pick it up. There next to my sweater stood a brown dachshund wiggling its tail and beside it our forest ranger. "What are you doing so far away from home?" he asked me and picked up my sweater for me.

"Anni and I wanted to see some blue lights," I replied. He stood in front of me, so tall I had to look way up. He smiled at me.

"Well," he said, "did you see some blue lights and where is your invisible friend Anni?" he asked. I shook my head so hard it made my pigtails fly from one side to the other. "Anni got scared and left," I said, pointing at the hiking trail. He took my hand. "Let me take you home," he offered with a kind smile on his bearded face. Happy, I walked beside him and told him everything Anni said about my mother.

"Some people speak out of ignorance. Don't pay much attention to it," he said. "I like your mother. She is very intelligent. If the world had more people like her, it would be a better place."

It was getting dark as we approached the house. Mother was waiting in the open door. I knew she would be mad at me for returning so late. "I probably have a lot of explaining to do," I whispered.

"Don't worry," the ranger whispered back. "I will put in a good word for you." Gently he squeezed my hand, and I squeezed his back.

While mother and the ranger greeted each other, I took the chance to sneak unnoticed into the house. One look at my dear

*Me, pushing my
doll around.*

brother and I knew I was in deep trouble. "Where have you been? Mother got even mad at me for not watching you better," he said. I ate my cold dinner still waiting for me fast that night and hurried up to the bedroom. Mother was still talking downstairs to my new friend the ranger. Later she came into my bedroom. "So it looks like you learned a lesson today," she said before she gave me a goodnight kiss. It was clear to me the ranger had done what he had promised. Now Mother was no longer upset with me. Well, I had lost a friend in Anni, but therefore gained another.

DENTIST APPOINTMENT

Being the only man in the house, Martin was happy, summer vacation had ended and so had the multitude of chores around the house. Elisabeth had returned from Berlin and a lot to report. Only Hiny still was sick with the mumps. That again left me all alone at breakfast time fighting the lumps of my milk soup. Mother was writing to Father. "Why don't you show him how nice you can write your name," she suggested, pushing the paper across our table. I dipped the pen into the ink jar, but when I pulled it out, it caused a large spot on the page.

"Don't worry," she just said and being super creative, she drew little matchstick lines around it and called it an ink sun. "Now get your color pencils out and write your name." I picked the brightest red I could find, but instead of my name I drew a little girl playing ball all alone under the ink sun waiting for her Daddy. While I drew, Mother hurried to get her morning chores done quickly, because we needed to walk to our neighbor village for her dentist appointment. I had only been there once before, when she pushed me in my stroller. Martin had to have a tooth pulled. I remembered the dentist as a very kind man. He gave us each a large apple to take home.

It was a long road to Reichenbach. By the time we got there my feet were aching, I was tired and hungry. When we got to Dr. Morgen's house we were shocked. Wilderness surrounded that once so beautiful mansion. Two large words were written on the white house wall. Mother said it was an ugly word for Jews. We found another sign on his front door "Property of the Third Reich." Before we left, we heard the next door neighbor call us over to her fence.

"We all thought he was one of us. He was born in our town and christened and he was a fine neighbor and dentist," she said. "But apparently he had Jewish roots. They came one day and took the whole family away."

Mother was shocked to hear such news. The lady wiped her hands on her large apron. "I picked all his apples before they spoiled. Let me get you some of them." She rushed into her house and returned a few minutes later holding a basket filled with delicious looking apples. "He was always so proud of them," she gave Mom the basket. "And this one is for you," she said smiling, reaching into her apron pocket and handing me the largest apple I'd ever seen. We thanked her and I curtsied like Mother told me to. Just before we left, Mom turned to look at that picture of devastation as if she still could not believe it. I know she was crying, because from time to time she kept wiping off her glasses.

"I guess my tooth will have to wait until the war is over. Hopefully our dentist will be back, since he is the only one for miles around," she said. "Let's pass the bakery by, on our way home."

Sweet pastry sounded much better than any dentist office. For a while I walked barefooted next to her until we came to the marketplace. Along the side of the street, we saw several men working with picks and spades. All of them looked dirty and skinny and one of the old men looked at me. Because he smiled at me so nice, I walked toward him trying to give him the apple I carried. We still had a whole basket full of them I thought, while someone screamed loud behind me. I turned and saw a woman in uniform, holding a rifle pointed in my direction. I was wondering if Mother wouldn't have stepped in front of me, which one of us she would have shot—the old man, the apple or maybe me? The guard still kept screaming about arresting and about disobedience to the law. And all the time it was not clear to me what kind of law I had been guilty of breaking. Mother was pulling me away as she was apologizing. We crossed the street and entered the bakery. The store owner offered Mother a chair.

"We have been watching through the curtains," he said. His wife brought Mom some coffee and pastry for me. "Sometimes we cook potatoes in their jackets and put them among those 'rocks' where the prisoners have to work. Then we keep the guard busy with coffee and pastry, so the men have a chance to find and eat them," the baker's wife told Mother.

"We always wished we could do more, but it is not possible," the Baker said. Even though we were their only customers, they sort of whispered each time they talked. They told us that one of their relatives had been arrested, just for listening to a foreign radio station and that our government killed patients in sanitariums for crippled and retarded people because they wanted to close them down. I believed they had more horror stories to tell, but we were interrupted by new customers.

"Thank you so much for your business and have a pleasant day," the baker said, handing Mom a sack with rolls and pasties she had not paid for. She thanked him. He answered with a loud "heil Hitler." Mom just raised her arm, but didn't speak. We left the bakery.

Me and my doll.

"It is high time for the Lord to make an end to this unrighteousness," Mother said on our way home and sighed. I could hardly wait for the kids to come home from school, so I could tell them all about our trip to Reichenbach.

"We can thank God, He has a few good people here and there," said Mom and I thought of that nice bakery couple, while we enjoyed eating their rolls with our homemade butter and raspberry jam.

CHANGES

My playmate Hiny was up and around again. He looked a little pale and had to wear suspenders to keep his pants from falling down, but I was positive all the good food in our house and the usual flour lumps from my milk soup would help to paint his cheeks red again. Each day around noon we waited for the mailman. We'd run and open the gate for him, so he could get through with some of those large packages my aunts sent from the Baltic. Mother said they contained valuable things my aunts sent to us for safekeeping, in case they had to leave their home. Mother stacked them unopened against her bedroom wall.

The weather was changing. It was mostly cold, windy or rainy. One of our favored places had become the kitchen window. It was the perfect place to stay warm and dry and still watch all those strange things traveling through our town lately. Mother called them refugees from Poland. Wagon after wagon, sometimes in long lines and sometimes isolated, were traveling west to safety. Some were pulled by horses and others by slow-moving oxen. I liked the uncovered wagons, because I could see all the things they had loaded. I saw wooden crates, trunks and large baskets stacked on top of hay next to furniture and cages full of chickens, geese and ducks. Small livestock was tied to both sides of the wagons and small herds of cows and horses followed along the sides and behind. Cats sat on top of the hay, while the dogs followed along the sides. Once in a while someone stopped in front of our garden gate because they needed tools and other necessities, but mostly food and water. Most of the people came from Poland, fearing for their lives because of their German roots. I was glad Mom could understand a little Polish and communicate with them about their needs.

One evening it was already dark when someone knocked on our front door. It was a farmer from the Polish border who was seeking shelter for a very sick man. Mother and Martin helped to partially walk, partially carry the sick man into our kitchen. He was a prisoner of war given by the German government to farmers who needed help during harvest time. Because he was very ill the kind farmer brought him along with the hope to find some medical help along the way. But now the weather condition forced him to seek shelter. "But of course he can stay," I heard Mom tell the farmer, who couldn't believe he finally had found someone with courage like Mom. Harboring or helping a prisoner or Jew was against our law. The farmer was planning to drop his family off at some relative's, return once more to his farm and pick up the prisoner on his way back.

"This might give him a few weeks to get better," he hoped, thanked Mother and left.

"He must have had a large farm," I said, watching him drive away being followed by a long line of wagons and a large herd in the pale light of the moon. But Mom was not paying a lot of attention to what I said. She kept busy with telling my sister and Martin all the things she needed to make our new guest feel comfortable. While Mom rushed around, creating room for him in our pantry, Elisabeth fetched Father's pajamas and other items while Martin went upstairs to get the mattress out of my big brother's bunk. He dragged it down the narrow dark staircase and I held the kitchen door wide open for him. The prisoner leaned in his chair, as if he wanted to slip off any minute. Traces of blood were all over the front of his shirt from coughing and he gazed feverish into the distance. Mother said the pantry was the best place for him, because he could get some heat from our kitchen and was also closet to her bedroom. It was perfect for keeping an eye on him during the night. The only problem was that our pantry was small and without a window. For air circulation the door had to be kept open. Mother's idea to sew a curtain and install it in front of the door was perfect. After Martin helped Mom to get our house guest situated, it was bedtime for all of us. She didn't have time that night to tuck us in, because she was busy feeding and taking care of the sick man and sewing the curtain. As I went to bed, I felt the warm towel-covered brick under the covers and pushed it down to my feet. Suddenly I heard the bedroom door squeak. Martin wrapped into his blanket sneaked in.

"I have been thinking," he whispered, "what's so funny about it all. Mom always busts us for lying. Actually now we have to lie, in case someone should ask any questions about our new house guest. She would have to thank us, instead of spank us." We all started to snicker.

"You better leave before she finds you in here and busts you for that," Elisabeth replied. After Martin had left, I laid awake a long time listening to the rhythm of Mother's sewing machine. I thought about what Father would do, if he knew his enemy was sleeping in his pajamas and what would happen if Hiny's father, who was in the SS, would ever find out anything about our visitor.

Me in our front yard.

GOODBYE HINY

Snow had caused the closing of our school. By the end of February it opened again. The children had to stay in school longer, to make up for the lost time. Finally the mailman delivered packages again. Some were our Christmas gifts from my aunts. And with the slow melting of the snow we watched how the long lines of refugees traveled westwards. Even people from our village began to move. One morning Mother and I just got through with breakfast and discussed my first school dress, when we were interrupted by a noise coming from the back of the kitchen. We stared at the door as it slowly opened. It was Hiny. He didn't say anything, just stood there in the open door with a strange expression on his face, carrying a bag. I gazed at Mother who looked as if she had seen a ghost. A million thoughts all at once crossed through my head. What if he had seen who was sleeping in our pantry? Hiny's father was with the SS. If he found out about that sick man in our house, Mother would go to prison and what would happen to all of us children?

"Why didn't you use the front door?" Mother asked him more nervous than angry.

"Because it was locked," he said, defending his action. "I wanted to surprise you."

"I hope you didn't go into our pantry. Remember I told you I put the pickle barrel into the front entry for you." Mother looked at him intensely.

"I didn't go in, I just peeked behind the curtain, but it was too dark to see anything," he replied.

"Thank God," Mother whispered, so only I could hear it, and

sighed relief to calm down. Hiny walked up to the table and pointed at his bag.

"My mom said we can't take all this along, so I just give it to you." He pushed his under lip forward, as he always did when he was about to cry.

"You mean your family is leaving, too?" Mother asked surprised, and I just sat there with my mouth wide open, staring at him in total unbelief.

"Maybe we leave this evening." He hung his head way down, so I couldn't see his face. "This here now is all yours for keeps, OK?" He looked so sad it brought tears to my eyes. He reached deep into his bag to pull out his precious three-legged horse with a half chewed-off tail and put it on the table in front of me. I watched him hugging his little brown Teddy a long time for the last time. All the nights he had spent with these hand-me-down, half squashed-to-death toys, and now leaving them with me, was an enormous sacrifice.

"Don't worry," I said, hoping to make him feel better. "I'll keep everything until you return." I knew how much he loved his little bed companions. Suddenly he must have smelled something, because he kicked the bag under the table, climbed up on the chair next to mine and viewed our potato pancakes with applesauce left over from breakfast. Apparently whatever was still left in the bag didn't seem as important at that moment as what was to eat on the table. He smiled all over his face as he watched Mom fix him a plate.

"Eat all you want, Hiny," she said, "especially since it is your last time at our house." Watching him eat, I hoped he would never have to be like the refugees passing through, seeking food and shelter.

"When are you leaving?" asked Hiny.

"We decided to wait a little longer. Who knows, maybe the war will be over sooner than we think." She put another pancake on his plate.

I pointed at the pretty fabric, still draped over Moms sewing machine. "Look," I said. "Mom's making me my first school dress."

But Hiny didn't show much interest in girl's fashion. His eyes, hands and mind concentrated on all the things on the table he could stuff into his mouth.

Suddenly we could hear the prisoner coughing. Quickly Mom banged around with a few pots and pans by the kitchen sink, hoping Hiny would not identify where the sound was coming from. As soon as his plate was empty Mom pushed him gently off the chair and toward the door.

"You better run along now, and tell your mother I'll be over later to say farewell." He left sadly, turning around at the door, looking back at me and the toys he'd left behind and his empty plate.

I pulled my chair next to the window to watch him leave. He didn't hop and skip like he usually did. Holding his head way down, as if he was moping, with both hands in his trouser pockets, he walked slowly, from time to time kicking a stone or stick.

He had been like a younger brother to me and a great playmate. And now he was leaving. At the gate he turned around waving at me, and I waved back smiling. And as he walked slowly down the

Our house in the winter.

street, the morning fog began to take him from my view. "Hiny," I whispered, and no longer bothered to hold back my tears. I looked at our sandbox. Without him I could close down our mud cake bakery. Nothing would be fun for me anymore. And what would happen if our secret, my brother's cracked ski tip, would one day be discovered? We had promised each other to share the punishment. But why worry now. Perhaps one day we could play again like we used to do. But for now all the fun with Hiny would have to be only a memory. His little Teddy was still sitting at the table. I picked it up and hugged it.

A SCHOOL DAY

With summer's end I finally had become a school girl. As much as I had been looking forward to this time, I now didn't feel happy at all. It was because our first grade teacher, a pillar of love and patience, had been forced into an early retirement. Mother said it was because she refused to join the Nazi party. The new teacher we had was young and very strict and Mother was afraid some of her fanatic beliefs in the Third Reich would rub off on us. "Are you ready now?" I heard her asking me with my head hanging down. I was brushing my "seaweeds," as she called my hair, because it was thin and straight. Flipping back my head, I turned to face her. There she stood, tall as a giant and straight as a candlestick, waiting to braid my hair into pigtails. She was holding two white ribbons in one hand.

"Today, if anyone should ask you what the colors of our flag are, you just look at your black and red checked dress and remember your white bows in your hair," she said, smiling down at me. Mom didn't mind our flag or its colors, but she complained a lot to have to raise her right arm to say "heil Hitler" each time she greeted someone. Once she pulled me on her lap and spoke about a time before I was born, when people could still greet each other any way they pleased, just as they still did in our Bible group. "But you must not tell anyone about it," she'd say. "Our Bible group keeps it a secret." Her voice had become a whisper and she looked around, as though she expected someone to be standing and listening. I promised to keep it a secret by simply nodding my head. "Don't forget to be polite to everyone," she reminded me, as she buttoned up the back of my dress. Then she helped me buckle my backpack. It was old and handed down to me from my oldest brother Ernst. Thanks to Elisabeth who had poked a few more holes into the straps, it was no longer slipping off my shoulders. Martin made fun of me saying it was because I was born with droopy shoulders and his best friend Guenther told me to add a few bricks to keep it from slipping. I would have enjoyed walking each morning between my brother and sister, but our new teacher had changed the school time and now class for me started one hour later. But somehow I was glad, because now I didn't have to hear how spoiled I was being the baby of our family, and it gave the big kids space to act and speak as they pleased, without being worried I would tell on them.

While Mother went down to the cellar to get me an apple, I took a quick look out of the window to see if the neighbor's geese were in sight. But the fog in our valley was still too thick to see that far. Before I left, I peeked through the crack between the pantry curtains to see if the stranger was still asleep. The last few nights he had not been coughing as much as when he arrived. I hoped he was on his way to recovery and be gone by the time Father came home again. Mother had returned from the cellar and was polishing my apple on her apron. After she added it to my school lunch, we folded our hands while I said my prayer: "Lord bless my leaving and my returning, bless all I do and all I say, bless me when I'm dying and grant me eternal life." I felt Mom's hand on my head and after she straightened my pigtails, I was on my way.

Running through the front yard, I could hear my lunch and first grade book rattling around in my backpack. Carefully I opened and closed the gate to keep it from squeaking so I would not alert the neighbors' gander, who had it in for me each morning—listening, watching and waiting. Slowly and with utmost care I crept along the shrubs on the other side of the street until I reached the always open gate of Sempert's farm. As soon as I spotted something white moving in the fog, I started to run as if Satan himself were on my trail. Hissing and honking loudly, the long-necked monster came half running, half flying behind me. In a few more yards I had safely reached the end of the farm. That was usually how far the gander would chase me. Only a few angry honks followed me as I jumped across the narrow brook. Catching my breath I rested a few minutes sitting in the meadow, watching the gander parading and still honking around self-importantly. In the distance I saw Dieter waiting for me at his backyard gate. His hair was as blond as mine, but short and straight and brushed back. His shoes were shiny but squeaked with each step he made. He liked to talk about his father who was spending time at home to recover from a war injury. "Guess what," he said, as I came closer, "my dad had that couple that's living across the street arrested." Proudly he walked beside me, waiting for my response. I felt a funny feeling rising up inside of me, but kept on walking and looking at the path in front of me. It was the couple that came to our Bible meeting each Sunday afternoon at brother Liebig's house. "Well?" Dieter asked me. "Don't you want to know what they got arrested for, or did you know all along they were hiding a dirty Jew in their house?"

"A Jew?" I acted surprised. "I had no idea they were doing that. How did your Dad find out?" I asked, not bothering to look at him.

"That is only for me to know. My father thinks we should have all the members of that little religious gathering investigated."

"Well, there isn't anyone else living in our house but us," I said, lying through my teeth. Dieter was now walking in the grass because the path was getting too narrow for both of us. I thought it was very polite of him, leaving it all to me.

"My dad said it would just be a routine check," he bragged.

"Just wait until my dad hears about that!" I shouted, pretending to be angry. "Remember my dad outranks your old man."

"I know your Dad can be trusted, but what about your Mother. She is an outsider and known as a peculiar person." He grabbed my arm and forced me to stand still.

"Let go of me," I was close to tears. "My mother loves our country. She would never do anything to hurt anyone."

"Then why are you crying?" His face was so close to mine, I could smell the liver sausage he had for breakfast.

"Because...Because you're hurting me." With these words I jerked away from him looking at the white imprints his fingers had left. He noticed it and mumbled some sort of an apology. Thank God Irene and Claus had caught up with us. Both were wondering what we were fighting about. Dieter tried to explain. And while I walked behind them, I could hear all about Dieter's old man being such a wounded hero, who was still working and cleaning up our country by having traitors arrested.

By the time we got to school, class had started. Fraeulein Mayer first walked around to inspect. She smelled so clean, as if she spent most of her free time inside a bathtub full of perfume. She had short legs that looked extremely fat. To hide them, she wore long and wide skirts. Our class had given her the beautiful nickname "Powder Puff." She made sure we would sit straight and any student who forgot to remember got a slap on its back to be reminded. Her best talent was to find something wrong with everyone. Only Dieter was an exception.

"Tell your mother to shorten your bangs and try to keep your pigtails out of your face," she said, while passing me. One boy sitting across had to go wash his hands, another got the stick for chewing on his nails. "Children are the future of a country," she would always say, quoting Hitler's speech, "and I will make sure our Fuehrer can be proud of you. And why is Mary looking under the bench?" she asked.

Mary lifted her head, all red in her face. "I think, I believe I seen a mouse," she stuttered, pulling her skirt down over her knees.

"Did that mouse run under your little skirt?" With the help of her stick, the teacher lifted Mary's skirt, not just to expose her always slipping stockings, but so much more. Totally embarrassed

Mary began to cry. "I believe I told you yesterday to have that fixed!" the teacher shouted. Mary had to stay after class to play with her invented mouse and another girl was sent home to return with her neck washed and her ears cleaned.

"Dieter my boy," Fraeulein Mayer patted him on his back, "I heard the good news. Our Fuehrer can be proud of citizens like you and your family." She pointed with her stick to the large photo hanging on our classroom wall of Hitler shaking hands with little children. Dieter locked his little sausage fingers as to a prayer, his cheeks all red up to his ears, looking at him as if he was God himself.

After recess our teacher was ready to make an important announcement. First she spoke about our forest and mountains, our rivers and lakes and how special and beautiful our fatherland was. She said our land was like a mother nourishing and caring and needed to be honored, even our soldiers died for it. She said how important unity of a family is and mentioned our first biblical parents Adam and Eve. It was after they both disobeyed God, they hid from Him. So if someone had something he hides, means he could be guilty of disobedience. She stressed the importance to keep our ears and eyes open. If we should notice somebody is hiding something, we should immediately confide in her. I thought about the stranger in our pantry we were hiding. We all promised to keep it a secret. He was a sick man who couldn't hurt a fly. The announcement was over. Our teacher walked through the classroom, looking at everyone.

"Why are you so red in the face?" she asked me.

"I, I need to be excused," I stuttered, hoping she could not read my mind.

"Why didn't you ask me sooner?" she asked suspiciously.

"I was afraid to interrupt that important announcement," I lied. She seemed to be satisfied with my answer, nodded her head and gave me a smile. I took off like a weasel. In the outhouse I took a break. I sat on top of the wooden lid, sucked my thumb and thought things over. I wished now I never had become a school girl. I liked learning, but it was those other things that began to scare me. The sunlight squeezed through the cracks in the door and lit up a big spider web hanging in the corner. And there was the spider, hiding and waiting to get its victim. I used one of my sandals to squash it into the wooden wall. Even in the outhouse, one creature was trying to make a trap to hurt another. As I walked back to the classroom, I knew I had found my very own nickname for Powder Puff. It was "Spider."

After class was dismissed, I waited for Martin and Elisabeth. Just before the other up-town kids joined us, I had time to tell them about Dieter's Dad.

"Don't worry," Martin said. "Our Father could make trouble for Dieter's Dad, if he should order an inspection of our house."

"Best you keep your ears open and your mouth shut," my sister said, before she took my hand to go home. It felt good walking between them. Just like my hospitalization, soon all this would become just a bad memory. While Martin and some boys chased after a frog, I stuffed my backpack full of wildflowers for Mother. Up at the Sempert's farm I saw the old gander waiting for us. Martin said

The hill I used to go down with my sled.

he had a new trick to teach that gander a lesson. Hiding behind the boys, I waited for Martin to make his move. The monster finally came charging toward him. Stretching his long white neck and with its beak pointing straight at Martin. He waited until it came close enough to almost touch it. Suddenly my brother grabbed the gander by its throat, just below its head. Its crazy honks turned into a pitiful gurgle and its eyes bulged out. Martin spun it around in a circle and threw it high above the fence right into the farm yard. The rest of the geese scattered in all directions, honking like crazy as they watched the high and mighty gander coming in for a crash landing. We all laughed, watching the gander still being dizzy trying to get back on its feet and trying to keep its balance.

That day I admired my brother's courage and hoped to grow up to be just like him who stared danger in its face and got rid of it.

AUTUMN LEAVES

My once so big school dream had ended, since it stopped operating until the end of the war. Most family with children, as well as our Nazi teachers, had left town. When Martin mentioned he hoped the teachers accidentally took the wrong train east instead of west, Mother told him to take his evil thought back. I couldn't tell if he did, but he mumbled something to himself while he left the room. "Look at my house slippers. My toes are always cold." I stood in front of Mother, pointing at my feet. My large toes had worked themselves through the slippers. "That can only mean you have two very nosy toes, or you are growing too fast," she replied smiling. "You better get dressed, so we can buy you some new shoes before the store closes."

To get a new pair of shoes was a special occasion. Usually I had to wear all the hand-me-downs from my sister. How perfect my day had started, I thought, while Mom took me to the shoe store. Mrs. Heller, the owner, was very helpful to select some good winter shoes for my size. She was in a hurry to close her shop. Many suitcases and wicker trunks stood by the door, waiting to be picked up. You can pay me after the war," she said to Mother, "if we are all still alive." She made some negative motion with her hand. Mom and her talked some more, while I went outside.

"Why is she suddenly so nice to us?" I asked Mom later, as I watched Mrs. Heller waving and smiling at us from the window before she closed the blinds. I remembered her as very unfriendly, especially toward kids.

"War can change people. It's that everyone is afraid of that uncertain tomorrow," she took my hand.

"But you don't have to be afraid of anything because I am holding your hand."

"What about you, Mom, are you scared?" I looked up to her, that tall strong iron statue who looked like she could endure any storm or any war.

"I don't have time to be scared, besides God is holding our hands as long as we ask Him to." I felt proud to walk alongside my mother. We all had someone we could trust in.

Our next stop was Elder Liebig's house. "You must leave," he urged Mother. "The Russian army is close to the German border."

"What about you?" Mother asked. Mrs. Liebig smiled gently while she served homemade bread with goat cheese.

"My wife and I are too old, we are ready anytime to meet our Lord," her husband said. He lifted up his head turning his foggy gray eyes toward the ceiling. "But you, you must do it for your children." He put his arm around my shoulders, as if he could see me standing there. I knew a lot of things tasting better than goat cheese. But with Mother beside me and this Holy Spirit-filled couple sharing their humble food with us, I washed everything down with Mrs. Liebig's delicious apple juice. Before we left, Elder Liebig made a very long prayer. Only this time when he said, "Lord Jesus come soon," I agreed nodding my head, because I didn't want the Russians to come first.

All the stores we passed on the way home had been closed. Only our butcher was still operating. Mother said his prices should be low, because of all the abandoned farm animals and all those weak and half frozen ones the refugees had left behind. Maybe he hadn't left town because this was his only chance in a lifetime to get rich. The only problem was, he didn't have enough customers. As we entered his store Mother noticed the prices had gone up instead of down. Being upset, she ordered only soup bones, some lunch meat and hot dogs. "It's wise to buy meat and can it for the long winter months ahead," he urged Mom.

"You are so right, that is the reason I canned all our rabbits," she replied.

"Preferring rabbit meat to all of this...?" the butcher shook his head. Mother paid no attention to what he said. I could tell it upset him. He threw his little hatchet so hard on the cutting block it overturned and landed on the floor. He wrapped our order in cheap newspaper and sat it on the counter with a loud "heil Hitler" and paid no attention to me standing there waiting politely for my very thin slice of lunchmeat he always handed out to us "future customers," as he called us children. On the way home, I thought how right Mom had been about people changing during war time. Mrs. Heller and our butcher were two people who had changed. What would war do to us? How would we change, and what king of ugly monsters would we meet next? At home we met the mailman. His kind and polite smile said he would never change, only his mail did. The letter he handed Mother was from one of her sisters. It said they were trying to flee by boat across the Baltic. Mother's voice was trembling and her hands shaky as she was holding the letter and kept reading. One of the latest radio reports had been about enemy planes sinking a large ship and many boats. Thousands of refugees drowned in the icy waters of the Baltic.

It was lunch. Mother fixed some of her sauerkraut with our ugly butcher's hot dogs, and I wondered how an unfriendly moneymaking Nazi like him could make such delicious tasting wieners. Martin was reporting the news our town crier had announced that our funeral home as well as our church were no longer operating. "That means no weddings, no christenings and if someone is ready to die he would have to wait until the war has ended," Elisabeth said and shook her head.

"Well, there is still Gustav who could help," Martin replied. Gustav was our taxidermist. He lived in an old house filled with stuffed critters. Some of them were attached to his walls and stared down with large glassy eyes. Elisabeth had just opened her mouth to speak, but Mother interferred calling it a bad "distasteful" joke, and we kept bending our heads low looking at our plates, until we could get those unwanted smiles off our faces.

"Who wants to go with me to the trout lodge?" I asked after lunch. Because no one cared to join me, I grabbed my cape and took off running all the way up the street, until I finally huffed and puffed like an overworked locomotive into the backyard of the trout lodge. All the outdoor tables and chairs were covered with a thick carpet of leaves. I climbed upon one of the tables to get a better overall view of the place. No children were in sight, only a few squirrels played around on the branches of a large oak tree. My legs dangling off the table I sat there just waiting and watched the wind blow the leaves to the ground. They reminded me of all the people, which war and fear had forced to leave, and now were scattered all over the west. And the bare branches looked like all the empty abandoned homes. But there were still a few stubborn leaves fighting, refusing and clinging still to their branches. Just like Mother, I thought, and some other people being strong, not giving in to the circumstances.

I looked around. Each year after summer tourist season, this large backyard used to be a place of fun and laughter. All the village kids would gather and throw each other into the large piles of autumn leaves. We would play catch or hide and seek. Sometimes Mrs. Jaeger handed out homemade cookies or flavored sparkling water or call for her maid, who loved to spend more time in the coach house than in the kitchen. There used to be familiar sounds, like the banging of pots and pans coming from the open kitchen window. There was no more barking of hunting dogs, no more hammering from the closed-up barn across the yard, only silence surrounding me. The place I had enjoyed most this time of the year, suddenly gave me the chills. Even the squirrels had left. This unusual silence caused a strange feeling to creep upon me. The narrow hiking trail leading into the pine forest looked suddenly dark and spooky. This place of fun and laughter had turned into a scary place without life. I heard the window shutters squeak. I did not bother to turn around to see if it was caused by the wind. I was stricken by an unknown feeling of fear, jumped off the table and ran like someone was chasing me. I felt as if this ghostly silence had changed into an invisible monster, chasing and scaring me, following me out of the lodge.

I had run as far as Marie's mountain. The light in the window of the little brick home at the foot of the hill helped my painful heartbeat to calm down. I slowed my steps and sighed relief. The terrible feeling of fear began to leave me. Old Mary seemed to be at home. There was smoke escaping her chimney. Thank God for signs of life. I wanted to knock on her door to say hello, but her large tiger-eyed cat sat on the steps staring at me, making me feel uneasy. There was the large steep hill behind her house. All winter long everyone would meet here all bundled up with sleds and skies. Sometimes old Mary stood in front of her door, lifting up her wooden cane she walked with. Some said she was waving and some said she was scaring the children off if they came too close to her dwelling. Passing by the deserted homes it seemed to be a ghostly silence walking

My mother, siblings and I.

with me. Little wooden crosses marked the small graves of their pets in the yards. People had been advised to kill them before they left. Finally our house came into sight. At least there was still life and a warm kitchen waiting for me. "There is no one left out there," I said, while hanging up my cape. I could tell Mother was glad to see me home again.

"How about a baked apple with all the trimmings?" she asked me as if she had read my thoughts and I smiled nodding my head.

"Mom, do all leaves fall off a tree, every single one?" I asked her later, eating my apple.

She nodded. "It's the rule of nature old things have to go to make room for new life on the trees. But there are exceptions like pines or cedar trees, which always stay green."

Maybe there was hope. From that moment on I just had to believe our family was one of the exceptions in nature and never have to leave.

THE SOLDIERS

By the end of September our village was slowly turning into a ghost town. The once so beautiful gardens had turned into wilderness. But it was not long until the early snowfall began to cover it all with a clean white blanket. I was wondering why I couldn't feel the usual joy that came along with the snow. All I did was sit at the window, staring and waiting—not being sure what I was waiting for. I just knew all the people who had left town had taken along the joy and laughter and the fun winter had for us kids. Only cold white silence was left behind and a strange feeling of fear. A few sparrows fighting for bread crumbs and long lines of refugees were the only signs of life outside our house.

Time after time our mayor had urged Mother to take us west, but each time she refused, finding excuses. Only we knew her true reason for staying was the prisoner. We all still hoped and prayed for either his miraculous recovery or for the farmer to return, who had dropped him off and promised to pick him up again. Several times our dear Dr. Wagner offered Mother to once in a while look in and see after the man's needs. But our doctor was old, the snow high, our house without heat and Mother felt responsible to keep her promise.

With the accumulation of the snow the nights were colder. Snowstorms forced the traveling refugees to seek shelter. That was why Mother kept light in one of our windows shining out toward the street, even though the rules of war required homes to be in complete darkness so enemy planes could not notice them. Everyone was thankful for this small sign of love shining for their rescue as they stumbled half frozen and hungry over the doorstep into our humble dwelling. Each time, Mother was more than happy to share everything we had available to help them. Night after night our home turned into a regular campground with blankets all over the floors and clothes lines stretched throughout the kitchen to dry the wet garments and diapers until the next morning. It highly upset our poor kitchen stove, because it made strange noises as if it was ready to explode and its top turned from black to pink fighting this abuse. In a short time it burned up a large supply of our prepared firewood for the winter and also the food in our cellar began to shrink considerably. Mother and Martin took turns chopping some more wood in that cold shed. This left Mother hardly enough time to clean up the house between these many nightly visitors. Mother kept Elisabeth busy peeling and cutting vegetables and I had to help with the dishes.

Some of the German-speaking refugees would talk about their beautiful castles, all their wealth and farms they had to leave behind. For the first time in my life I watched men cry like children and ghostly-looking faces staring as if their eyes could penetrate the walls. Those were people broken in spirit, who had slipped out of their royal garments and put on a robe of poverty, sleeping under a blanket of hopelessness and being afraid to wake up in the morning fighting for survival. Even the children seemed so different from us, shy and withdrawn they somehow kept to themselves instead of playing along with us. Only the babies kept their bright smiles and happy faces. I laid awake in my bed thinking, wondering about life and people and wished for the end of war and things to change back to normal. It was in the morning when we found out something had changed. Our house was infested with three different plagues. We had head lice, fleas and bed ticks and with the stores being closed, we had to live in this terrible condition. Mother, who was a very clean housekeeper, was totally devastated and felt betrayed for her warmhearted hospitality. But each night, when the icy north wind whistled and wolves howled in the nearby forest, she didn't have the heart to turn anyone away that knocked on our door.

Finally one afternoon Mother's prayers had been answered. The farmer returned to pick up the prisoner. Immediately Martin rushed to the office of our mayor to tell him we were ready to leave. But he returned with the bad news—we had missed our last chance. Like most years at this time we had been cut off from the rest of the world. Trains were no longer in operation. But Mother would not take "no" for an answer. "Where there is a will, God will make a way," she said, selecting strong canvas and turning it into four large travel sacks, which she stuffed with important survival items and lined them up side by side in our entrance, ready to travel. There was still hope one of the covered wagons could take us along at least for a distance, until we could reach a train. But in vain we waited for someone to travel through town. Cannon fire woke us up during the night. Behind the hill the whole eastern sky was glowing red. Scared to death I spent the rest of the night sleeping next to my sister. The following day we waited for refugees, but in vain. I sat by the window, my favorite place since Hiny had left, thinking about Father, Ernst and wondering where everyone would be. Suddenly I saw something move in the distant snow. I wiped the window glass for a better view.

"Mother!" I screamed. "The Russians are here!" I could identify five soldiers walking slowly down the street. Mother, who had kept busy hiding the last of our aunts' packages under the floorboards of our attic, came half flying down the stairs. We all crowded together looking out of the window as the small group came closer. My heart was beating totally out of place. I had the feeling at any time it was jumping out of my throat.

"Those are our soldiers," Martin was sure about identifying them.

"Yes, they all look like Father," Elisabeth jumped up and down with joy and my heartbeat began to slow down.

"Germans!" we all screamed in one accord and ran to the door. By the time Mother unlocked and opened they stood there, all five of them.

"Thank God for you," Mother said overwhelmed with emotions. "We first thought you might be Russians."

"The smoke from your chimney can be easily spotted from quite a distance," one of the soldiers said pointing at our stove, leaning his rifle securely in the corner behind the door. "You never know, we might still need it, the enemy is close behind us."

Martin and Elisabeth helped our guests out of their boots. Mother kept busy heating up some stew and made hot tea for everyone while each of the soldiers took turns cleaning up in our cold pump room. Later I had to sit on everyone's lap hearing how much I reminded them of their own children, who they had not seen for years, and listened to the stories of war and survival. They had been able to hide during days and walked by nights. Germany had lost the war, but our radio was still lying—we were winning on the eastern front.

"We are only soldiers by uniform. Actually we are more like scared running rabbits," one of the soldiers said.

Mother had to do a lot of explaining why we had not left yet. We had a long evening together, sitting there in the company of five wonderful scared rabbits. I felt as if life had returned to us.

We were no longer alone and neither the nightly cannon fire nor the cold white winter silence scared me anymore.

I woke up in the morning listening to all the noises and voices and it was as if new life was pulsing throughout the entire house. I was sure those five scared rabbits had been sent by God as guardian angels for us. It was after one of the soldiers, the highest in rank, went and had a long talk with our mayor that we were promised to have one more chance to leave. He returned with the good news to be ready to travel in the afternoon. We had no more time to say goodbye to anyone. From now on it would be only prayers that would connect us. Mother laid out my clothes to dress for the trip. By the time I got dressed, I felt like one of my stuffed toys. The soldiers prepared a very special lunch for all of us. It was a roasted goose with potato dumplings and sauerkraut. Mother did not ask any questions about the goose and I hoped it was Sempert's mean old gander.

As promised, an army truck stopped at the gate to take us west. The soldiers carried our luggage and helped us into the truck. Everyone had an encouraging smile and tears in their eyes as they hugged us goodbye. They promised Mother they would wash the dishes and turn our house key into the mayor's office before they left. I sat on one of our sacks looking out of the back of the truck to wave at them for the last time. We knew them only for such a short time, but I felt as if we had left half of our family behind. When the truck made a strong turn, I landed on the floor and rolled over to Mother. Because of all the clothes she had made me wear, I couldn't feel any pain. Mom sat on a piece of luggage, leaning against the truck.

A Sunday walk to our Lookout Tower.

"It is good to lean or hold on somewhere," she advised me. This was my first time I sat in a motorized vehicle. I sat on Mom's lap so she could hold on to me. We had come to the end of our village. Smoke escaped from the Liebig's chimney, there was the deserted school, then the church and a few more homes. Soon it was out of my sight. What would happen to us now? When would we return? Would we see Father and Ernst again and what about my aunts, Hiny and all the rest of the people we knew? I looked at our sacks. That was all we had left from our home. We had now become victims of war, one of those people Mother had given shelter to each night. We were now refugees.

"Mother," I asked, "where are we going?"

For a few minutes she looked at me without saying anything. Then she held me close and pointed outside the truck. "You see that beautiful world out there? We go where the Lord takes us," she whispered. I couldn't see her face, but I knew she was crying.

LEAVING HOME

This army truck wasn't moving very fast. All the roads were heavily snow packed. The chains around the tires played the music to our journey. I leaned against Mother. We both still sat on top of our sacks. The two brown sacks Elisabeth and Martin sat on reminded me of stuffed long sausages fit for a fairy tale giant. They were discussing all the things they planned to do, as soon as we would return. Home was now quite a distance away. There was our little house with the warm kitchen we had left behind. I could almost smell the roast goose the soldiers had prepared for our last meal together. Hopefully it was the mean gander they had served. Maybe from now on, if we ever should return, I would not have to be afraid to get chased on my way to school every morning by that white long-necked monster. The soldiers probably were through washing the dishes as they had promised Mother and left our house. Hopefully they took her advice and used our skies to travel. Of course mine, being only one yard long, had to wait until I came back. Maybe now I could forget about that cracked ski tip and instead thought about the soldiers who had been such a help to us during these last days of fear and worry.

Each time the truck made a strong turn I would have slipped off my seat, if it wouldn't have been Mom's strong arm holding me back. I thought about our Nazi teacher and her sneaky ways to try to get us kids to say something bad about our parents. Maybe after the war things would change like Mother once said and school could be fun again. I wondered if our house would still be standing and all the many treasures would be still in place that Mom and Martin had been hiding under the floorboards of our attic. But the things

I liked most, not even a million wars could destroy. It was the wild flowered meadows, our deep dark pine forest full of raspberries and mushrooms and the snow in the winter. "Do you think the Russians will throw bombs on our little house?" I asked Mom.

"Our little house," Mom said smiling. "The Lord will see to it that it misses their attention." It almost sounded like she gave an order. "I have a good idea for all of us. Let's sing, it will chase sad thoughts away," she suggested. Only this time no one felt excited to sing as we usually did while walking through the beautiful countryside. It used to be fun marching to the rhythm of the music. Mother began to hum the folk song about the Linden tree, and we finally all began to sing along. Martin remembered his harmonica, a Christmas gift from Ernst before he left for boot camp. He pulled it out of his backpack and played all three verses. Even though the melody as well as the lyrics were sad, it somehow made us all feel better.

Suddenly the truck began to slow down and came to a stop. We could hear many voices and crying of children. The driver opened the canvas. It was evening and too dark to see the faces of the new passengers. Our truck filled up in a very short time and after a few more stops we felt like a bunch of canned sardines. Each time the truck made a strong turn, people fell into each other. There was a lot of complaining but no apologizing. It all turned into heated arguments, until a strong voice of a man made an end to it. He announced if anyone kept it up they would have to exit at our next stop. It felt like being in a classroom with naughty children. It only took one strong voice of authority to create silence.

At the following stop people refused to crowd together any further. "We smash our children!" one of the mothers cried out.

"Everyone out," the driver's voice was loud and angry, "including your luggage." Everyone crawled out and threw their suitcases and trunks in the snow. Martin helped Mom pull our sacks out of the truck.

"Now each family boards again with only two pieces of luggage. Lives are more important than possessions," the driver announced, having found a solution to the problem. Immediately people began to complain. Some of them even cried, because they could not remember what important items they had packed in what suitcase. This caused some to lie and cheat, saying they were divorced. "If you can't show me the necessary documents, you count as one family with two pieces of luggage or you do not enter my truck." The driver had spoken, holding one hand on his gun to make everyone obey. Soon we found ourselves packed together again and this time, everyone sitting on their luggage creating more space. Giving up their possessions caused people to be unhappy. There was a combination of ugly odors from baby diapers, smokers and garlic eaters causing people to complain. Someone said he felt like a clean shirt among dirty underwear and one of the ladies said, "Let's find that clean shirt, so we can throw it out of the hamper." There was moving and pushing going on, and children started to cry until suddenly that strong voice of authority again called for peace. Only this time it did not work. At the time when everyone had to get out of the truck we found out it belonged to a short man with a mustache. "Listen to that Hitler talking with his big voice of power," someone made fun of him. His remark struck the nerves of some fanatics among us and if it would have not been for all the mothers and children between the men, it would have caused a regular battle. The man next to us reminded me of a chained-up mad lion and his wife of a lion tamer calming him down. I was not sure which side he was on.

Suddenly we heard a lot of explosions seconds apart. And then we could hear planes charging down so low it sounded as if they flew right above us, flying back up, only to return again and again. The driver had stopped our truck. People opened the canvas. With the lights off, we were parked under some trees. In the distance the sky looked like it was on fire. The city we had just left was being bombed. Some wanted to leave the truck and others held them back.

Everyone seemed in a state of panic. Praying, crying and cursing people surrounded us, until the sounds of planes began to fade away. Our truck began to move again. People had stopped complaining and fighting. Maybe everyone was happy to be alive.

It was not long until we stopped again. The driver came and told all of us to leave. He had received new orders. "If you stay on this trail, it will take you to the train station. You should get there in about ten minutes," he said, pointing in a certain direction. One of the men complained about carrying his trunk on that icy road. But the driver had no time to listen. He jumped into his truck and took off. We all stood there in the dark of the night, in the snow. Mother picked up the sack we had sat on and carried the large milk container wrapped in a blanket containing our food. I walked behind her and Elisabeth and Martin lined up, carrying our other sack. We all had our backpacks strapped in place and started to walk, looking like a bunch of hobos going on a trip. People began to argue again. In the dark someone had picked up the wrong luggage. "Keep on walking," I heard Mother saying. It was not long until we could see the light of the train station appearing in the distance.

THE TRAIN

It started to snow again. I held my head way down to keep the flakes out of my face. Each step we made creaked under our feet. "I hope the trains operate in this kind of weather," I heard Mother say to Martin. Both were leading our little family troop. I was lucky their heavy sacks and backpacks slowed them down enough so I could keep up with them. Sometimes Mother forgot I was only six and my legs a lot shorter than hers. The three pairs of socks made my shoes too tight and my toes numb. Elisabeth and I walked close behind them. Wearing two sweaters over several blouses and my ski jacket on top of my overcoat plus my backpack, made me as stiff as a board. Mom's idea "we can't lose what we are wearing" had sounded so good but now felt so bad. It kept on snowing. I was sure Anna was full of snow. It was my favorite doll peeking out of the top of my backpack, so she could see everything going on behind me.

It was a strange feeling knowing we now also had become refugees. I remembered the ones who had traveled through our town all these weeks. At least they had covered wagons stuffed with possessions, but we only had what our backs and hands could carry. Hopefully the war would soon be over and we all could go back home. Maybe the group of soldiers had been right saying our government broadcasted nothing but lies by announcing on the radio that Germany was winning in the east. Before we left, Mom and I was feeding our rabbits for the last time. She had torn out the partition to the next stable where Hans used to live, until Father made a meal out of him during his last furlough. We stuffed the empty stable full of carrots and potato peels. Mother left the door wide open, but the gray-furred rabbits had no idea what freedom meant. Overwhelmed about all the food we gave them and the open stable door, totally confused they cuddled up against each other, hiding in the back corner of their dwelling. Somehow I was glad we didn't have any other pets. How painful must it have been for our town's people to silence their loyal companions.

And finally our little troop had arrived at the Breslauer train station, a large dark gray stone building with huge glass doors and a wide staircase leading up to it. We had to stand in a long line of people and wait our turn for tickets. There were people as far as one could see and birds flying around in a high dome ceiling. Finally I could feel my fingers and toes again and Mother smiled holding our tickets. It was only a short journey through a dark tunnel, up another long staircase to board the longest train I'd ever seen. I heard someone say it was the last train transporting refugees out of this part of Germany. Half pulled by my brother and half pushed by Mom, I landed on one of the passenger wagons. There Martin had still found a vacant compartment that was seating six people. A musty odor surrounded us but the upholstered seats looked extremely comfortable.

"I feel like a stuffed toy," Elisabeth said, pulling off two layers of her extra clothing. So did Martin and soon both sat comfortable in their seats while Mother was still outside the train, waiting for someone to load our sacks into the luggage wagon. I still stood there not being able to bend my arms.

"Anything wrong with you?" Martin looked at me somewhat amused and snickered. He knew good and well what my problem was without me having to explain anything.

"You wouldn't need our help?" Elisabeth's voice sounded super sweet. I had been standing there like a clay statue ready to break out in tears, but now their sarcasm brought out my stubbornness. I lifted my head to swallow my tears.

"I'm waiting for Mother," I replied, but not being so sure of it, since I felt the urge to use the bathroom. They just looked at each other and grinned. At the next compartment a lady stuck her head out of the door. "Why don't you help your little sister?" She looked into my mad red face, still holding back my urges.

"We are trying to teach her to ask for help," Martin said.

"And to say 'please'," my sister added.

"Well?" The lady stared at me waiting. That did it for me. I was sick and tired of people always trying to tell me what and how to say things. I was always expected to plead and crawl and just because I was four years younger than my sister and six years younger than my brother. That lady had no idea what my life was all about. I was the fifth wheel on the wagon called immature and stupid. Go and suck your little thumb, everybody said. No, I rather would wait for Mom or stand there until I died with my backpack on wetting my six pairs of panties I was wearing.

Of course having that much pride and patience was later highly rewarded by Mother, who finally relieved me of all my torture and jumped all over my siblings for not helping me sooner. My brother had to give me his window seat. I finally felt like smiling again and Martin and my sister had to be nice to me again, at least in the presence of Mother.

I used my sweater sleeve to wipe the settled steam from the window to get a better glimpse of the platform outside. "I am glad we came early!" Mom said, looking at all the people still waiting to board. Old people were sitting on top of their luggage, waiting for someone to help them, little children, some crying being carried or pushed in strollers and ladies wearing expensive fur coats and high heeled boots, who tried to keep from slipping. And through all this confusion someone maneuvered a large luggage rack, a shelf on wheels stacked with sacks and crates, suitcases and traveling baskets. Some people wore Red Cross bands around their top sleeves, helping the very old and invalids to board and carry some of their baggage. One of them was holding a crying child, looking and searching for its parents. And there I saw someone I knew. It was Mrs. Becker.

She lived in our village near the school. She was speaking to a train conductor who was shaking his head while pointing to a stretcher being lifted into one of the luggage wagons. Mrs. Becker sank to the ground. Red Cross people rushed to get her up and half carried, half walked her to a passenger car. I grabbed Mom's arm. "They just loaded Becker's Walter into the luggage wagon."

"Maybe they set up a space for crippled people," she tried to calm me down. "I'm sure his mother is with him." I shook my head and told her everything I'd seen. "That does not sound good," she grabbed her overcoat. "I better check this situation. Luggage cars usually don't have any heat or other conveniences." But she never made it to the door. A whistle blew, a small jerk and the wheels under us set the train in motion. A voice over the loudspeaker announced for people to step away from the now-moving train. Upset, Mother hung her coat back up and sank into her seat. "Lord, help that boy," she whispered, taking off her glasses and wiping her eyes. I still stood at the window. She smiled and pulled me toward her, giving me a big long hug. Both of our thoughts were with Walter in that cold, dark place among the luggage without his mother. And I had the feeling, as if that extra tight hug Mother gave me was meant for Walter.

THE KLINGERS

Our train was not a usual train transporting tourists and people taking a nice trip to a nice place, it turned into a half of a nightmare. Everyone had lost possessions and now being forcefully fenced in together they were losing more than that, they were losing patience, pride and dignity and most of all their temper. Every few minutes the conductor had to be called to settle arguments and fights between families. But there was not much he could do to help them. This time it was an elderly couple that refused to split up and sit apart. The search ended with the still two empty seats in our compartment. It made an end to take turns to be able to stretch out to take a nap.

Mr. Klinger was not just a very tall man but when he took his seat next to Martin his enormous compact figure squashed my brother further into the corner next to the window. His smile was more of a friendly grin when he shook hands with Mom introducing himself. His fat legs a mile apart touched Martin's bony little knees. He reminded me of a giant in my fairy tale book who ate little children for supper. I was glad Mother had wrapped our large farm milk can, which was standing next to Elisabeth on the end of our seat, looking like a rolled together large blanket. It contained all our jelled rabbit meat Mom had canned during the year and now had taken on the journey to a place unknown to us. Across from her next to her husband sat Mrs. Klinger. She was a short lady with a huge chest size who would not take off her overcoat. The strange thing was, each time the couple spoke to each other it was more like a whisper.

I stood at the window watching the world outside passing us by with white-covered meadows, sugarcoated trees and icy ponds. Only once in a while I saw an isolated estate in the distance and was wondering if the owners had to leave them behind like we had to do. Soon I could see nothing but trees. Some of their low-hanging branches packed with snow came so close they almost touched the window. I felt sleepy and sat next to Mother, leaning against her arm, sucking my thumb. Mrs. Klinger kept wiping the sweat off her forehead. Even Mother was wondering why she did not take off her heavy overcoat in this warm compartment and finally asked her. As if she needed help to find an answer she looked at her husband. But Mr. Klinger was deep asleep, whistling out of one corner of his mouth. Turning to Mother she explained having only one coat and being afraid it might disappear while she slept. Noticing her nervousness, Mother took her excuse for an answer.

It was not long until everyone had fallen asleep besides Mrs. Klinger and me. I was trying to figure out what was wrong with her chest that she kept rubbing from time to time when it started to wiggle. The light had been turned down but I could still see her sticking sometimes two of her fingers between the coat buttons to calm down her nervous chest. That's when she looked at me and I could tell she was not happy with me watching her. So I closed my eyes and pretended I had fallen asleep. Suddenly I heard a tiny voice saying "meow." Opening my eyes again I looked at her and smiled. "A sweet kitten" I thought and now knowing her secret, I fell asleep.

When I woke up, it was already daylight. The constant sound the train wheels made on the tracks was a regular lullaby. Mrs. Klinger's overcoat was now nicely folded laying next to her. The sweet kitten I was expecting to see had turned into a large pile of black fur and laid half covered up between Mrs. Klinger and her coat. No longer could the couple keep their cat a secret. Pets were not allowed on this train. But after we listened to the most unusual story how this black ball of fur had one night saved Mrs. Klinger's life when she had a nonstop nose bleed, we understood their feeling for this hero.

Next was our turn to reveal our secret that was still untouched hiding inside the blanket. To keep their cat a secret, Mother agreed to be kind enough to share equal portions of rabbit meat with the couple. Only Mr. Klinger did not agree to it. "A man is entitled to a larger portion than a little girl," he demanded and the cat also needed to be fed. I could tell Mother was upset. We not only had to share our food, but also our spoons and cups we ate with. We knew if only one word would seep out, it would have been our first and last meal. People had not thought of this train being without a dining car and now had to find out it was only transporting refugees.

MISSING HOME

I was tired looking at nothing else but trees passing by the train window while I listened to Mr. Klinger complimenting Mother how good his large portion of rabbit meat tasted. Next he asked Martin for some of our bread he carried in his backpack. When Martin told him that there was none left he had the nerve to grab the backpack open it up and stick his long red nose into it. We all smiled on the inside because we knew Mother had taken it out while he slept, and broke it into large equal pieces so we could hide it in our jacket pockets.

Martin left our compartment for some time to spy. He returned with the good report that at our next stop food would be available for everyone. When the train finally rolled into a large station people were facing a great disappointment. What we found was a soup kitchen with a sign "bring your own container." Most everyone had containers, if any, packed away in their suitcases, which were stored inside the luggage wagons. People fought each other to check the garbage containers of the train station for empty beer bottles, which was not accepted by the lady who handed out the soup.

We were standing in line waiting with our two cooking pots Mother had given us to be filled while three girls in front of us argued with the woman who refused to fill up their bottles. Two of the girls began to cry. That's when Martin handed them one of our cooking pots. After we had returned and confessed what had happened to our second pot it made Mr. Klinger highly upset having to split one pot of soup between all of us. Later my sister and I took our dishes to the bathroom to wash. Like usual there was a long line ahead of us. If someone took a long time people would bang against the door. Children crying, some people cursing, some screaming at each other in different dialects was always on the daily schedule. Glad to be back in our compartment, I played with my doll while Elisabeth and Martin played checkers on top of Mr. Klinger's suitcase that he allowed them to use as a table.

Soon we had left the city behind us. I felt sorry for all the people who didn't get any soup and thought how nice it would have been if they would have handed out pieces of bread or hard rolls as well. Now I was standing at the window again, gazing outside, dreaming about home and wondering what had happened to all the people who had not left. I hoped our rabbits would still be alive and someone would pick all the wonderful raspberries and mushrooms.

Mrs. Klinger returned from the bathroom saying it was now made "out of order"—no paper and no more water. From now on we had to use the one in the next wagon standing in a longer line of people. Her husband loved to brag about that beautiful mansion they had left behind and wanted to know more about us, what kind of house we owned and what rank my father had in the army. I could tell Mother felt like we were being investigated. And when she hesitated with her answer I told him our house was called "The evening star." That made Mom smile and Mr. Klinger satisfied. What he did not know was that people made fun of our little house standing next to a large and wealthy mansion called "The morning star" and had made up a nickname for ours. But it caused his mansion to get bigger and better each time he talked about it until his wife gave him some angry looks.

Leaning onto Mom I drifted off to sleep. Being awakened from a strange jerk I noticed our train had stopped. We stood in the middle of nowhere and had no idea why. This happened more often and sometimes it took almost one half day until the train could move again. Finally we heard from the conductor we were traveling in a war zone. Sometimes our tracks needed repair and sometimes they just needed to be cleared and checked. Now we had the answer for some of the smoke we could see in the distance.

One night our train slowed down again until it came to a full stop. We could hear the sounds of sirens and suddenly all lights went off. Next we could hear the roaring of planes coming closer, diving and explosions over and over again. The forest looked dark and spooky but the red sky told us a nearby town was under heavy bombing. Thank God our train was hidden in the dark of the night and the large trees. We got the message it would take a long time before we could enter the partially destroyed city. The train would give us three loud warning signals to tell us to be on board. Everyone was happy. Now we had a bathroom to use as long and wide as the forest and we had a lot of nice snow to clean up with. We picked the icicles off the tree branches and chewed like one does on lollipops and while Mr. Klinger with wife and cat were roaming outside, Mother handed out the last of our rabbit meat. When they returned Mrs. Klinger was in tears. Her cat was missing. We all went outside to look for her without any success. Her husband gave her hope by saying there is still a lot of time until we leave.

It was late in the evening when Martin had to tell us that a few men were talking among themselves about how good a cat actually tasted, just like rabbit meat. They laughed and meowed. We all kept this to ourself and hoped Mrs. Klinger would never find out what happened to her hero.

MOTHER'S DECISION

Mrs. Klinger's eyes stayed red and swollen. Her husband complained because she was using up all their hankies and Mom could not lend him any of ours that we used mostly as wash rags. Somehow I had the feeling he was not too unhappy about the missing cat. He no longer had to feed the cat from his portion of rabbit meat. When he found out that we ate it all while they had been roaming around outside he was highly upset and accused Mother of cheating.

It was two days later when we heard a warning whistle, then a second and later a third. It gave everyone time to board the train. It was going very slow, one could have jumped on or off. We could see a lot of destruction and the streets were filled with homeless people—some pushing and pulling small carts filled with luggage and children. Many times we stopped because they checked the tracks for possible damage. It took a long time until we reached the next city.

It was afternoon when our train stopped again in the middle of the open countryside. We had no idea why or for how long. Downhill we could see a large pond. Since we had finished our food, Mother had no longer been hiding our can. Now everyone was voting to send Martin to fill it up with water. Mom was against it out of fear to lose my brother. People begged and mothers cried because there was no water to clean their babies or dirty diapers. After Mom talked to Martin she finally agreed if another boy his size or older would take the risk to help him carry the large heavy milk container. Soon another boy was found to join him. We watched how they ran downhill and filled up the can. Mom with her hands folded was praying silently. By the time the boys made it halfway up the hill we heard the first whistle blow. The other boy began to run while Martin was still holding onto the heavy container. He carried it all alone until the next whistle blew. He let the can roll down the hill and started to run for his life. He had almost caught up with the boy when the third whistle sounded and the train went into motion. We watched and prayed hoping the boys could jump onto the train until suddenly trees took them from our sight. Now we had to wait until our next stop. The luggage wagons at the end of the train prevented the boys from coming through. It was only one half hour that seemed like an eternity until we saw the boys again. I never knew until that moment how much I loved my brother and I believed he felt the same way. Only a few people were glad to see the boys back, the rest complained about them dropping the water. It was the thanks Mom received for having compassion and she made the decision that this would not happen again.

AUSTRIA

Everything had improved. Our train had picked up speed again, no more destruction or traveling refugees on roads as far as we could see. Someone spread the news we were coming close to the German-Austrian border. From now on we guessed that our destination would be German-occupied Austria. I heard Mother mention that this might be our last day on the train. Mr. Klinger seemed to be in a better mood, Mrs. Klinger had found comfort holding her rosary praying for her lost cat and I had the feeling that her husband's attitude about my thumb sucking had improved.

It was late afternoon. We had crossed the border when our train stopped at a large city. People with Red Cross bands on their arms pushed large containers on wheels through our train to hand out sandwiches. On fruits we could choose between apples or pears. For me that was a good sign of things to come. It took a long time to hand out the right luggage to each family and split us up in smaller and larger groups. A farm wagon with modern rubber tires pulled by a fancy tractor took us to a refugee camp in Heizing, our destination. I could not believe my eyes. The three girls from the soup line and their mother belonged to our small group. The third family was a young lady and her father who spoke Polish. It was not long until we stopped in front of the restaurant in a small village. Our friendly smiling driver whose German was overpowered by a strong Austrian accent helped to carry the luggage into the building. In a very long and wide hallway with many doors he pointed to the first at the right. It was one of the restaurant's dining rooms, which was being used as a temporary shelter for German refugees.

From now on we had a new home, two bunk beds with a space of approximately one yard between. All beds were pushed against the walls throughout the room. A cooking stove in front of the back window and several pushed-together tables with benches had to be shared among us. Our first meal was provided by the restaurant owner as a welcome. We promised Mom we would be on our best behavior, friendly, honest and polite. The owner, a very friendly elderly couple whose strong Austrian accent was hard to understand served us a traditional dinner. Of the noodle dough dumpling covered with a well-tasting meat in brown sauce Martin could not get enough and the owner kept smiling at him reloading his plate. Our dessert, a large piece of apple strudel with a cream sauce was followed by "Most," the traditional Austrian cider drink in place of our German beer. Mom kept her eyes on me so I would not drink too much of it. While Elisabeth helped the lady to carry our empty dishes back to the kitchen her husband gave us a lot of information. This was the only restaurant in a small farm community. There was no school, no church, no police or fire department, no doctor or hospital and only one store carrying goods for farmers. Besides sharing the outhouse in the back of the residence we had to come up with firewood and our own meals. It was expected to keep peace among us refugees and not steal or destroy anything. The next town to shop was called Aschach at the Danube River and located about one hour away.

After paying the outhouse a visit we sneaked into the already dark camp and not to disturb the sleeping refugees we went to bed in the moonlight shining through the high windows. It felt so good to be able to stretch out my long legs. Mother whispered a prayer with us and made sure we were covered. And while I watched the moon painting silver trims on the snow around the window frame I thought about the most beautiful evening we had since a long time.

GETTING ADJUSTED

It was early when Mother woke me. "Maybe you don't want to wait until you have to stand in line for one hour," she suggested. I dressed in a hurry and ran out to the backyard. The line in front of the outhouse was still short. Only a few people stood in front of me. To prevent me from listening to their conversation they switched to Polish. Everyone who came after me kept pushing me to the back of the line saying, "Little girls can go behind some bush or barn." Finally I was in tears and had no choice but to run behind the large barn. I was looking for something I could hide behind when I noticed a small side door partially open. When I peeked into the large barn full of hay and straw, I knew I had found my very private outhouse.

It was later when Mother wondered what had taken me so long. I told her about the hay and the egg nests I had seen. "I hope you did not touch them," she said, "those belong to our landlord." Before she walked all the way to Aschach shopping she went to check with the landlady if she would sell us eggs, milk or bread. That's when Mom found out she had promised her husband not to sell any food to the refugees because of all the chickens, the eggs and potatoes that kept disappearing. When she asked Mother if she would be willing to work for food, we knew it was an answer to our prayers. Mom's seamstress talent had now become our blessing. Mother took Martin and our empty sacks to the faraway wood to fill them full of pine cones and sticks to fill up the half-empty wood box next to the stove. The following day when it was our turn, after most of the refugees had cooked their stolen food, they had used up our firewood. Knowing that Mother worked for our food made them angry and when they found out that Mom was allowed to use the large restaurant stove it turned them against her.

It was not long until we noticed the three evils that had infested our camp. In addition to the head lice we received from the refugees who had slept in our house we now had picked up a certain kind of cloth lice and bed ticks. Because of the dirty condition in our camp it had spread like wild fire. Mother could not find anything in the stores to rid ourselves of these three evils. As long as the snow lasted we pulled the sheets from our beds and hung them around our bunks to make a private corner to wash up and look at each other's heads and clothes to kill lice and their eggs. Poor Martin was elected to do the guard duty. All refugees besides the three girls and their mother came from the German-Polish border. The women wore long wide skirts with several petticoats and kept their long thick dark hair in buns or tied braids pinned up. Never washing it made it a perfect nest for breeding more lice. The bottom of their white petticoats had turned black and needed mending from sweeping the ground and we never saw them washing anything and hanging it up anywhere to dry. "Maybe they are so deeply depressed they are not able to function normaly," Mom said when we wondered about such a behavior.

Thank God we had one large bowl that we had to use for washing ourselves, our clothes, the dishes and the floor. We also had to use it to prepare the food. The bad thing about it was, we had no soap or detergent of any kind and often no hot water to clean it well.

The young lady living with her aged father and her baby in one of the bunks on one side of us was too lazy to wash diapers. She trained her little boy, who just had begun to walk, to use our territory to perform his nature calls. For those occasions she had stripped him nude and after he had committed his crime, called him back. The first time Mom took it for an accident and cleaned it up. When it happened again she called the young mother to do the job. She came with a straw broom and kept wiping everything forward and back until it worked itself into the untreated floorboards to leave behind a large, brown stinking area for us. That's when Mother had to use our "bowl for everything" to clean it up. From that time on we pushed and walked the boy over to his territory each time we noticed him coming around the corner.

One day one of the families in the back of our camp moved their old grandmother into the empty bunk bed next to me and my sister. She always slept with all her clothes on. It was morning when I heard her talking to herself. I looked down from my bunk and watched her pull her sheet back. It was white, covered with little black polka dots. I remembered the hospital and the bed ticks, which our soldiers had carried along from the field hospitals. It was not long until they found her dead and after Mom helped prepare her for the funeral service she told us the poor woman was covered with infected tick bites and sores. That's when she came up with the idea to ask the landlady for a few sticky fly trap hangers. We helped her adjust them to the floor between the bunks hoping those crawling evils would be forced to take another direction. Next Mom talked to the mother of the three girls who had their bunks on the other side. But she showed no interest while sitting on one of the benches smoking and waiting to be picked up for her next date. We felt sorry for the three girls who kept to themselves. Many times we had tried to make friends with them without any success. We tried to find the cause. Elisabeth thought it was pride, I voted for shyness and Martin topped it off with being plain stupid. Mother did not say anything. She was just shaking her head each time another man came by to take their mother for walk.

Christmas had come very sudden—unexpected since we had no calendar. Everyone spent the evening in church. Being Lutherans we had the whole building to ourselves. With candlelight, singing and praying Mom handed out some apples, cookies and candies our landlady had given to her. Before we turned in we talked about home and made plans for the future. Later from my bunk I could see a few decorated branches of a Christmas tree in the window of the house across the street. I snatched one candy to chew and stuffed the rest deep into my pillow case. I thought about the holy evening back home, my dollhouse, my aunts' packages under the beautiful tree and most of all about our Christmas dinner until I could almost taste it.

MAKING FRIENDS

On the third floor of the restaurant lived a little girl named Annie. Each time one of us tried to speak to her she ran away and screamed, "Mother, Mother, the Germans are trying to kill me!" But that all changed when we met by mistake inside the large gray barn, which we both used for the same purpose. We looked at each other and laughed, knowing we both were partners in crime. That's when she invited me to play with her beautiful dollhouse. Because she was only four years old it was easy for me to convince her that dolls could eat if no one watched them. She divided a whole tablespoon of sugar among the dolls and by the time she returned from the kitchen with some chocolate milk powder it had already disappeared. Only a few sprinkles had remained on the tiny plates and on the lips of the dolls. Of course the bigger the dolls, the more they ate like cookies and apples, which I cut into nice bite-size pieces. To overcome my guilty feelings fooling Annie I helped with a few chores like washing dishes and sweeping the kitchen floor. I hoped it would prevent her mother from being upset if she heard about the hungry dolls. But my happiness lasted only a short time. After the snow had melted, my sweet sugar paradise closed its doors. Annie and her mother moved to a town providing schools and church.

It was not easy for Mother to come up with enough food for our family. Martin was six years older than I and could devour a whole horse and I was always looking for something to eat. Mother said I was growing too fast and many times she gave us her share with the excuse she was not hungry or she had already eaten. The still unripe grapes that climbed up the gray barn wall and the traditional growing cider apples gave me a bad bellyache until I came up with the idea to offer my help to the young farm couple across the street. I was happy for the small job they gave me to take the baby each afternoon for a long stroll. The cookie or candy I received as pay was not as satisfying as I had hoped for. So I became inventive and took little Loni with her stroller to the back of the barn. It was a nice quiet place with high grass and wild flowers, shade and privacy. There I spread out her blanket. But before she could take her afternoon nap, we split her baby bottle full of fresh creamy cow milk, leaving a satisfying buttery taste in my mouth. Since Loni was a regular overly nourished butter ball with hamster cheeks I felt like I only did her a favor by sharing. Each time it was my turn to drink, I unscrewed the nipple. Remembering the dishwater without detergent covered with one-half inch of grease made my stomach turn. Poor Loni had no choice and I felt bad sticking that ugly, smelly slimy nipple back into her mouth. It did not seem to matter much to her, she always had happy eyes and a sweet smile kicking her legs into the air. And while I watched her drinking the rest of her bottle, I considered myself lucky she could only speak two words, Mamma and Pappa, or our afternoon crime would be revealed.

The warmer weather now gave us the opportunity to wash up in the creek next to the restaurant. To get clean we used sand for soap while the village children gathered across the creek laughing and making nasty remarks about us. Sometimes it caused a regular war between the refugee boys throwing wet German dirt balls against the village boys using Austrian rocks. That's when our family waited until almost midnight to sneak out and wash up by moonlight.

One night we had a terrible strong thunderstorm keeping everyone awake. I watched from my bunk how the women of our camp gathered around the table praying by candlelight holding their rosaries. Perhaps their extreme fear had something to do with pushing me to the back of the line at the outhouse, stealing our landlady's eggs and chickens and cooking them with Mother's firewood and being unkind to us. I thought how different and easy it was for me. I could talk to Jesus and His Father anytime anywhere without being afraid of punishment. I kept sucking my thumb and while listening to the mumbling and thunder—I watched the lightning flashing in the sky and knew that God loved us.

DAYS IN THE CAMP

Today Mother had planned to take us all on a shopping trip to Aschach. She assured us when we finished we could see the beautiful Danube River.

By the time we had reached Aschach my feet were hurting so bad, I had to take off my shoes. Martin mentioned they had been shrinking and laughed, Elisabeth said I had grown too fast and Mother came up with the idea to wear my good-fitting winter shoes in the middle of the summer. I sadly remembered all the nice "hand-me-down" summer shoes from my sister standing lined up in one row back home just wasting away.

What a great disappointment it was to see long lines in front of every store. Mother thought it was best to split us into groups. Martin lined up at the baker and butcher shops while Elisabeth and I took the long line at the milk and cheese store and Mother went to look for the Red Cross office to put in our name and address in case someone was trying to find us. Listening to some of the news at our landlady's radio we knew Germany had been heavily bombed and we had little hope to see Father and Ernst as well as my aunts from the Baltic again.

People kept cutting into the front of our line and by the time we finally got to the door they hung out a sign "closed for today." At least Martin showed up with a bunch of day-old hard rolls and some lunchmeat. By the time Mother returned from finding and standing in line at the Red Cross, most of the stores were closed. A little disappointed, carrying my shoes and eating one of those delicious rolls with heavenly tasting lunchmeat while wondering how long it would last, we were on our way back to the camp.

Tired from our trip we all rested for a while until the sky turned dark and we remembered our laundry still hanging outside. Mom's face was all red when she returned with just a few pieces. "Someone has stolen most of it," she explained. She asked some of the refugees if they had seen anyone out taking things off the clothes line. One of the old farmers admitted he only took off the things Mother had stolen. Now Mother explained that it was tradition for better class families to have their initials embroidered into all of their linens and underwear. A lot of them came from Mother's hope chest and some were presents from her sisters with their initials. The old man would not discuss it any further and told Mom to see if she could find any law for us to get her possessions back. It was another disappointment to find out the police would only interfere if an Austrian was involved. This situation was between two German refugees and it was our loss. From now on we had to watch the people walk around in Mother's beautiful slips they used as nightgowns, sleep under our sheets and dry up with our towels. That's when I wished God would send a few terrible frightening thunderstorms to scare them bad enough to return to us all the things they had ripped off.

AN INTERRUPTED NIGHT

Instead of my expected thunderstorms, we had so much rain the creek had turned into a small wild river. While washing our garments we had to be careful not to lose them and end up in the blue Danube.

It was naptime for me. From the top of my bunk bed I watched the wind blowing the rain against the window while listening to the growling of my stomach. Since Mother had caught up on her sewing job the landlady did not have much for her to do and that meant less food for us. Our meals had turned into very small portions and caused me to prowl around like an animal for food outdoors. There were the still unripe grapes climbing up the barn wall, the sour leaves that grew in the meadow, the watercress at certain places at the creek and the sour clover growing next to the moss around some trees. Sometimes I picked a few of those tiny green apples the Austrians grew to make their traditional cider called "Most" and chewed them to swallow the juice and spit out the pulp. What my mouth enjoyed, the rest of my system refused and with such a diet I had to stay close to the barn for emergency nature calls. I still dreamed of home, our large vegetable garden with fruit trees, and our forest full of delicious sweet raspberries and flavorful mushrooms. To this memory I held on like to a rescue rope only in time it got longer and longer.

Mother woke me up. The mailman had left a small package for me. It was from Annie containing a few nice apples, cookies and a tiny jar filled with a few tablespoons of sugar. There was a note that said she was missing her big "doll." I snatched a little of the sugar and gave the rest to Mother to split for all of us.

When I went to bed I thought about Annie and how sweet she had been making me think she had fallen for my trick telling her dolls could eat and how much I missed her.

A loud noise woke me in the middle of the night. It sounded like all of Austria was on an emergency move. Wagon after wagon rolled down the street, some pulled by horses and some by tractors. All were empty with only one driver. Mother as well as a few of the refugees went to investigate this situation. In a few minutes she was back waking up Martin who could sleep through everything and told him to dress in a hurry. The German Army had opened up a large warehouse for the public to take possession of all the food before the expected enemy would arrive. The neighbor from across the street took Mother and several other refugees along to Aschach. With his shoes in his hand Martin ran to catch up with them and jumped on the back of the wagon. Most everyone was excited and talked about what kind of food and how much they would return with. One of the women wore Mother's beautiful white flannel nightie. That made me stay in my bed discussing food with Elisabeth and dreaming about sauerkraut, stew and dumplings.

Hours passed. It was still dark outside when Mother returned. Martin carried a sack on his shoulder, Mother and the rest of the men who went carried in large boxes. "We will explain later," Mother said going back outside to get the rest. When she returned I could tell she was not in a good mood. "Several of my boxes are missing. This is all we have," she said pointing at two boxes and one sack. Now we heard what had happened. By the time they arrived at the warehouse most things had been taken. From what was left Mother chose several boxes of coffee, cigars, and hard sour lemon candy. There was no more food, only in one corner of the warehouse they found rice mixed with peppercorns spilled out of broken sacks. They were able to find a large sack and filled it up with what was left and Elisabeth and I had to volunteer to separate the rice from the peppercorns. Mother and Martin would go to the hills and trade the other goods for food. Only her two boxes of coffee were still missing. Each day I sat at the table separating the rice and looking at those thieves in the back of the camp—hoping for more severe thunderstorms to roll in.

A NEW FLAG

It was a sunny day. Mother went shopping in Aschach and took me along. Martin had left to get some firewood and Elisabeth had to keep a watchful eye on our bunk bed home to keep the thieves away. Shopping was always a struggle standing in line behind twenty or more people just to find out the item you needed was sold out. Like so many times before we managed again to get some day-old hard rolls and a baby formula we could use as powdered milk.

We finally started our one-hour walk back to the camp. I was already tired and hungry. My legs were hurting from keeping up with Mother. She was so tall, when she made one step I had to make two.

At the end of town we had to pass by a large restaurant. Mother noticed something had changed. It was the flag. Our flag that had been placed on the large flagpole since the German invasion in Austria had now been replaced with a new one. Mother said it was an American flag. As we came closer we could see the entire large beer garden was crowded with U.S. soldiers. For a few moments Mother stood still. Suddenly she took my hand and we walked through the open gate until we stopped at the first table. There a soldier sat in a chair slightly tilted back with both of his boots placed high on top of the table. Mother pointed at his boots asking him very politely to put them back on the ground where they belonged. She said it was disrespectful to the country and to its people. Apparently he did not speak German and sent for someone to come and translate. A few minutes passed until another soldier came to the table.

"He wants to know if you need boots or shoes for your family," he asked Mother in German. She shook her head and repeated her request. The young soldier seemed to hesitate to translate what Mother wanted. "Do you know you are speaking to an officer of the U.S. Army? Maybe you'd rather ask him for something else," he suggested. But Mother shook her head again and the soldier translated what she had requested. With a strange expression on his face the officer looked at Mother while he told the soldier to ask her if she was aware that we are still at war and if this is all she asks of him.

Mother answered, "Yes." Now the officer viewed me and Mom, his face expressing disbelief mixed with some sort of amusement and pity. Mother stood tall and straight like a statue still holding my hand. Carrying my shoes in the other I looked at my sore toes and feared he might order the rest of the soldiers to put their boots on all the tables. I knew we were a pitiful sight, a picture of poverty. Some of the soldiers had surrounded the table. Everyone was waiting for his answer. But nothing happened. There was only silence until he turned to the young soldier who translated again for Mother. "He wants you to know he will do as you asked of him, but not to honor your country, only because he admires your courage."

After that the officer removed his feet from the table. Mother thanked him with a happy smile and a handshake and I received a candy bar, which I took back to the camp to share with my siblings.

THE APPLE STRUDEL

Day after day my sister and I sat at the camp's, community table separating the peppercorns from the rice. The three girls kept watching us from one of their upper bunks. The package of hard lemon candy I had placed on the table finally made the girls come down and ask if we could use some help. Elisabeth and I agreed and told them they could chew as much candy as they wanted as long as they worked. Very eager, all three of them started the job while popping two or three candies at one time into their mouth. I knew it would only last until their mouth was getting too sore to chew another candy. And as I had suspected, the employment lasted only a short time ending with tears in their eyes.

In the afternoon, Mother and Martin returned from the trip into the hills. Isolated farms had traded food for cigars and lemon drop candy. On the way back they met some gypsies camping in the forest. Among them was a German refugee lady doctor who had a great supply of insulin. Because of all the bombing most of the medical industry had been wiped out. Medication was hard to come by. Mother knew our landlord was diabetic and trading insulin for food had now become a blessing for the doctor, for us and most of all for our landlord. The rest of the people who had stolen Mother's box of coffee she had brought back from the warehouse had not been lucky to be able to sell or trade it. Most of the farmers in our area had been able to obtain it themselves. They were much too lazy or some too old to go into the hills and address isolated farms. Therefore, several times a day our camp was filled with the aroma of fresh-brewed coffee. Perhaps they hoped Mother would trade some of our food for a cup of coffee. Only when we heard on the news broadcast that soon the war would be over, they once in a while began to offer Mother one cup of her own coffee.

One day our landlady asked Mom to help her make some apple strudel. Instead of money she gave Mother all she needed to make one for us. We helped and kept pulling the dough until it hung down over the card table like a tablecloth. We loaded it up with butter, apples, sugar and cinnamon, rolled it up and shaped it into a large circle. Our landlord offered to bake it in his large bread oven. To take it out he used a flat and wide shovel connected to a long stick. Martin and Mom carried it on a large tray into the camp. Everyone was invited to eat and we all sat around our community table and enjoyed that traditional Austrian delicacy and the thieves brewed a large pot of coffee as sacrifice for this occasion.

A few days later we watched covered wagons pulled by horses parking side by side on the meadow next to the farm across the street. Thinking these would be new arriving refugees we ran out to meet them. Some of the gathered town children whispered that these were gypsies. Their black hair matched their eyes. The older women wore black head scarves tied to the back of their heads while the younger ones had colorful ribbons braided into their untamed, long curly hair. They helped each other setting up their camp and spoke a foreign language. They had friendly faces and smiled a lot. One of the men walked up to me and touching my hair he said something I could not understand. His sunburned hand reminded me of leather. He smiled and I had the feeling he was admiring the color of my "sea grass," as Mother called my hair. Later on at sundown I watched them from my window as they sat around an open fire. One of the gypsies played a guitar-like instrument and sang. The melody reminded me of some of our sad folksongs. Even though I could not understand the words, I felt as if he was singing of all agony on this earth, longing for a way out. My heart understood and listening to his music made me feel I was not so much different from that gypsy.

Somehow our feelings of loneliness and loss and longing for a better world somewhere in this night air were meeting in his tunes. The only difference was, he was a gypsy by tradition and I had become one not by my own choice.

THE TRAP

Mother heard about a Lutheran church located several villages away. To take a shortcut cross-country walk the landlord had designed us a map. It would help us from getting lost. The following Sunday morning we started out early. Singing and marching behind each other on narrow trails helped to ease the long journey.

Several hours later we finally had reached the church. We quietly sneaked into the back just to hear the last song and the blessing. On the way out people passed the pastor shaking his hand. Suddenly I discovered Mrs. Becker from our village in East Germany. With tears of joy she hugged us. We all were tired from the trip and accepted her invitation to follow her to the farm that had given her shelter. The boys were happy to see us. With Walter being bedfast and Reinhard having epilepsy she had a hard life. For helping with farm work the landlord provided all the food. With eating and talking the time slipped away.

It was shortly before midnight when we arrived at our camp. One of the refugees met us at the door as if she had been waiting for us. "We have no electricity," she said, "the thunderstorm probably caused the blackout. But I have good news for you..." And she began to tell us our father had arrived. He had found us through the Red Cross. They showed him our bunk beds. He was so tired from the long trip and was fast asleep. "Maybe you should wait until morning to wake him," she mentioned.

Thanking her for the good news we sneaked in the dark to our bunk apartment and undressed in the moonlight. Dad was sleeping in Mother's bed turned toward the wall snoring loud. Mom reached under the bed to pull out the little box containing an emergency candle and matches. It was not there. Tired from the long trip I climbed up into my bunk happy that Father was alive and well and about the Becker's family I felt so sorry for. Father had stopped snoring. Suddenly I heard Mom scream and jump out of her bed. I looked down and saw Father getting out of bed as well. I remembered Father being almost one head shorter than Mother and was shocked to see this shadow of a fully-dressed man was a lot taller than her. I heard Martin jump down from his bunk and watched him chase that shadow out of the camp and down the street in the moonlight. It was not long until he returned, saying the man had disappeared in the dark. In the meantime we had listened to whispering and snickering coming from the beds in the back of the room assuring us it all had been a nasty dirty joke.

Before I fell asleep that night I thought about all that delicious apple strudel Mother had handed out so kindly. Now I wished it would feel like poison in their guts with hurting and puking and half killing each other running to the outhouse hoping to make it in time.

GOOD AND BAD NEWS

The good news had quickly spread. The war was over. All refugees were now waiting to be returned to their homeland. Home had carved itself into my memory as such a wonderful place. But now with arising questions it began to look like a paradise lost. Everything was bombed and destroyed. What would the bridges, railways, and train stations be like? How long would it take for all to be restored? Thinking of our village, would the houses still be standing and the people left behind still alive? Winter was not too far away. We could not plant or harvest. What would we eat and without firewood how could we survive that cold winter? "God will find a way to see us through," was Mother's answer.

While we patiently waited to be notified by the government to move, Mother once more walked to Aschach to the Red Cross office to see if there was any news about our family members. When she returned she had the answer to all our questions. Germany was now ruled by four nations. They had split up our country into four zones. The British had taken the north, the Russians the east, France part of the west and the Americans took the south and part of the west. If we could return to East Germany we would live under Communist law. We also could not return to our homes because Russia had handed our part of the country over to the Polish people. From now on all names of rivers, towns and places had Polish names occupied by Polish people.

All the refugees in our camp sitting around the community table had listened to Mother but no one believed her. Everyone agreed she was making up a story because she was seeking revenge for the nasty joke they pulled on her. That night while we prayed together she was crying. Until now we had been only homeless temporarily and now it had become permanent. I laid awake a long time wondering what would happen to us. Maybe we could live in the American zone. I remembered all the soldiers we met at the beer garden and the chocolate I had received. They seemed to be nice people even if they had bad habits like placing their boots on top of the tables. And I thought about all the food and things the refugees had been stealing from our landlady and from us. It was nothing compared to what the Russians had taken away from them now. It was their land, their farms and everything they were so proud of. It was almost heartbreaking. Somehow I felt sorry for them and I took back my wish for future thunderstorms.

Being unsure whether Mother had told the truth, people in our camp sent one of the men to Aschach the next day. When he returned, he looked gray in the face, shook Mother's hand and apologized. From that day on it became very quiet in the back of the camp. There was no more laughing, only red eyes from crying and once in a while a good cup of coffee for Mother.

Returning "home" was on my mind. Two things that I learned to love and knew I would never forget, was the landlady and her husband and the green hills of Austria.

COMING HOME ....

It almost broke my mother's heart when we found out our home was now under Communist law and my birthplace had become Polish. This forced us to settle as German refugees in the west of our own country, which was still occupied by the U.S. forces.

We had boarded the train filled with refugees from different camps and were now on the way back home. Martin and Elisabeth, my two older siblings, discussed with Mother the possibility of going back to school, while I stood at the window watching the country-side passing by. It was late summer, harvest season with busy people in fields and orchards. For the last time I captured this picture of perfect peace in the gallery of my memory, the blue water of the Danube, the green hills of Austria with snowcapped mountains in the background and its kind and hardworking people. But one thing I knew, nothing would ever replace our little house, the rolling hills, the deep fairy tale forests full of mushrooms and raspberries with tales of gnomes, giants and wood spirits, we had to leave behind. This, my place of birth would be forever carved into my heart as long as I lived.

It was afternoon when we arrived in the city of Nuernberg. There all families were put into groups. Our group was being trans-ported by trucks to a much smaller train station. Along the way we could see the results of war, which had left a horrible sight. Large places on both sides of the street had been bombed and turned large city houses into piles of broken bricks. Once in a while I could see part of a house still standing and staircases leading up into no-where. People in our truck just gazed with tears in their eyes and we thought about those that had been buried under all that devastation or burned in cellars while seeking refuge. I remembered our father, who belonged to a rescue team, telling us about saving people out of burning houses when the heat was so severe it had melted the tar in the streets. Wondering if he was still alive, we had to board a much shorter train to be taken to our destination.

After several stops a friendly conductor told us to get ready because it was time for us to exit. Going uphill, the train slowed down, making a strong bend. Mother helped me fasten my backpack and reminded us once more to be polite to everyone. We passed a few isolated houses until the train rolled into a small station and came to a stop. Tractors in front of modern open farm wagons with fancy rubber tires were waiting to transport us refugees. Martin and a few other boys were allowed to sit on the tractors. The kind man, who helped lift me and our luggage up in the wagon, explained to Mother we would be taken to a temporary shelter until the town found a permanent place for us. When I listened to the drivers speaking to each other, it was like a total foreign language. This dialect sounded ten times as bad as the one in Austria and I was not sure if I would ever be able to speak it.

It was slowly getting dark and began to rain. Mother made sure we sat on top of the long sack containing our feather quilt, blankets and our clothing to keep them dry. To our surprise it was a short trip and ended up in front of a large restaurant. Behind a beer garden filled with folding tables, chairs and large trees, light was shining out of the wide open door of the dance hall. The families that had arrived prior to us, now were now forced to move together to make enough room for several wagons full of us newly-arrived refugees. There gloomy faces and unkind remarks were an unexpected welcome. My sister helped mother spread out the feather quilt and one of the blankets next to the wall to mark our territory. It was then that we noticed all the large windows were packed full of faces of nosy village children staring at us, until I began to feel like an animal in a zoo.

Martin laughed, saying maybe we could charge them for sightseeing. Mother who had also noticed it, told us to smile at them and in spite of all, be kind and understanding. Elisabeth who had searched for bathrooms reported they were all inside, clean with lights and running water. In case of long waiting lines she had discovered some wild bushes growing along a narrow pathway leading behind the dance hall. Martin was left to stand in the long food line while my sister and I crawled under a blanket to change our wet clothing. When Martin returned, the lights had been turned off. After he had found us in the moonlight he unwrapped a big packet with a large sandwich and an apple for each of us. For half of my sandwich he let me have his apple, which I split later with Elisabeth. My own I stuck into my pillow case to enjoy it the next day for breakfast.

OUR NEW HOME

It was a slow process to find a permanent dwelling for all those many refugees. No one could tell us whether the government paid the rent or if it was up to people who volunteered to take us in. Farmers were looking for families with older boys to be of help to them. Our brother Martin, being thirteen, counted as a child. A widow with 6 children and our family were the last ones waiting. As much as my brother tried to make friends with some of the village boys, he could not understand their dialect and said it would be tough to get used to.

One evening a friendly lady came to pick us up to take us to the village castle, our new home from now on. We kids walked behind Mom and the nice lady. Martin told me not to get any ideas about being a princess. As poor as we were, they probably would make us live in the dungeon. The lady who picked up our conversation smiled and told us the castle had been built over 600 years ago and all the royalty no longer existed. After a few minutes we arrived. There it was in front of us in the moonlight—big, high and dark, like a monster waiting to swallow us. Passing the large entrance we walked along a stone wall up some steps into an old graveyard until we came to an iron gate. There we crossed a narrow bridge leading us over a large dugout, which surrounded the castle. From there we entered the backyard.

After we walked halfway around the gray sandstone building, we came to the back entrance. Inside the lady knocked on a door to ask for the key to our apartment. A woman's voice welcomed us with cursing and screaming until the door shut with a loud bang.

The friendly lady apologized to Mother and took us up to the fourth floor. The two upper floors were dark until the lady used a flashlight to find the two guest rooms we had received. Before she left she handed Mother the key and her flashlight in case we needed it to find the bathroom. Both rooms were small and narrow, each furnished with one bed with totally worn-out mattress. At the end of a long, dark hallway we found a small bathroom several steps into a super large dark attic and a staircase leading to a locked trap door leading into more attics and the castle tower. Next to the door leading into our first room we found an old rusted-out deep sink. Before we went to bed, Mother prayed and thanked God for our new home. It was nice to be able to wash up and undress without having the feeling someone might be watching. Suddenly we heard a loud noise. We rushed and looked out the window. It was the steeple clock of the church next to the castle and parallel with our window. From now on, each time we wanted to know the time, all we had to do was look out the window. My sister and I were sharing the bed in the first room and talking until she fell asleep. I was awake a long time listening to all the noises I heard, trying to identify them. I finally pulled the covers over my head, sucked my thumb and thought of Austria. There our home had only been two bunk beds with a walking space between them for almost one year, now we had two rooms in a castle and I was wondering why I did not feel happy.

THE CASTLE'S DRAGON
AND THE VILLAGE THIEF

For a certain length of time, a home that gave shelter to a refugee had to provide one meal per day. So each evening we marched downstairs into the castle's restaurant to receive our dinner. Not being allowed to choose our own table, the owner seated us in a corner out of sight from the other guests. Of course we understood we were unwanted and the way we dressed was not suitable for this occasion. We could not help to look like a bunch of outdated hobos and always hoped people could understand our situation. We would have been happy to wear handouts, but instead of help, all we received were dirty looks and laughs.

From the kitchen came a heavenly aroma of pork roast. And then SHE appeared, holding a large tray full of plates. She did not look much like a dragon, nor did she greet or say anything to us like the night we arrived. I still could remember hearing her cursing and screaming that evening. A hiding fire in her eyes told us how much she hated to be our waitress. In spite of everything our plates were loaded with steaming sauerkraut, roast pork and gravy plus a potato dumpling as big as a man's fist. She put my plate in front of me with a loud bang to give me the silent message that she hated kids! Being afraid to look at her I just whispered a short "thank you" while wondering how someone who cooks that good could hate so much. She left and returned a second time with salad and a glass of beer for everyone. Mother allowed us all just to take a few sips of beer with the meal. After we all praised her cooking, and Mother gave her thank you speech, nothing changed the hate that was written all over her face.

The next night Mother asked the landlady if she would be so kind as not to serve beer to us children. We could tell by the look on her face, she had taken it for an insult. Even though Mother tried to explain that we were too young for alcoholic drinks, she still seemed upset. The next evening she made her husband wait on us. They were a perfect match—unfriendly as she was and with a fake politeness, carrying his pride as lord of the castle like a crown on his head, holding his neck stiff as if he was afraid it could fall off.

The weather was changing and the nights were getting colder. Mother planned to warm up our two-room apartment with the large green ceramic tile stove, which was built into the wall and filled out the corner of the first room. It was not for cooking, but it had two openings that one could keep something hot. One side had a crossbar to hang up wet things to dry. For several days Martin helped Mother fill up and carry home two sacks with pine cones and sticks until the forest ranger made it possible to sell us firewood for the winter. Several days later Mother was asked to report to the mayor and was accused of being a thief. Someone had watched her and my brother cross a potato field with the sacks filled with pine cones, which gave the appearance of containing potatoes. After Mother explained that they took a shortcut over a field that had already been harvested and that we were too poor to own a shovel to dig, he apologized.

During the wheat harvest we went to the empty fields and searched for the fallen wheat tops the farmers did not bother to pick up. My feet had grown and I lacked shoes. Walking on those stubble fields was pure torture until we met a lady who came up with a helpful idea. She was a refugee who lived with her husband upstairs in the pastor's house. She told us to wait until dark and use some scissors and fill up the sacks by clipping off the tops of the wheat. She had done it many times and had never been caught. Mother did not agree to her perfect idea and said that God sees everything we do. That's when the lady walked off mumbling something that sounded like "stupid bunch."

It was not long after that when we heard the news that she had to move out of the pastor's house. She had been caught stealing. But this time it was not wheat but dirty shoes, which farmers after working in fields, left in front of their door to prevent soiling their house. A few days later she walked to a neighboring village as a traveling sales lady to sell the shoes she had cleaned and polished. After the war with all the factories and businesses being bombed, people did not mind to buy used things. She was happy to sell her stolen goods for food or money until the day she got caught. It happened when one of our farmers was visiting his cousin in the neighboring village and noticed he was wearing his shoes. The cousin, who remembered the lady, described her well enough. Since our town had no newspaper, only a town crier, we never found out what really happened to her.

SCHOOL TIME

It was time for my sister and me to enter school. Due to the refugee camp in Austria we both had missed one year. They insisted that I start all over with first grade. After a few months I was transferred to second grade, which was just moving to the other side of the classroom since both grades were together. Our teacher was not just old but also a bundle of nerves with a loud, high-pitched voice. I believe she did not know what it was to smile or to be calm. The only thing I found nice about her was that she used her stick only to point out things she wrote on the blackboard, never to punish us. Sometimes she waved her skinny arms in the air, but when upset she would touch us with her bony finger and leave a dark print on our arms.

Once every week we had one hour of religion. That's when we all separated into groups of Lutheran and Catholic and went to different classrooms. Looking down from the second floor, I watched the Catholic priest slowly climbing up the staircase. One of his students, while rushing by, greeted him with "Glory be to Jesus Christ" and received his answer "Forever, amen." I had never heard something so beautiful after all the many years of ugly "heil Hitler" that I felt urged to try it. I wanted to know what would happen though I was not Catholic. Going downstairs I passed him, and looking up to that tall, skinny, white-haired man repeated what his student had said. For a moment he stood still and recognized I was not one of his students. His face lit up with a warm smile and he answered, "Yes, forever amen." It made me very happy and for one moment I felt as if two souls had hugged each other.

During the war, industry had been destroyed and businesses bombed, therefore many things we needed were hard to get. Among those articles was paper, which was a necessity in every outhouse. I watched the farmers pump the sewer into their honey wagons and spread it over the empty fields. But the person in charge of the sewer of the school did not do a good job. Each time one opened a toilet lid, the sewer was so high that throwing in a small rock made it splash up. That caused the pupils to use another system. Our school outhouse was a long stretched building with one entrance for boys and one for us girls with a wooden wall between and also between each of the six stalls they had. The system the kids had invented when nature called was to fill out the many holes in the concrete floor or find a place in each stall without opening the lids. Hardly anyone used it during recess but asked to be excused during school hours. To find a solution for the missing paper, most everyone used the stall doors and walls to clean their hands on.

I never entered the boys' outhouse museum, but this building was a nightmare and the picture gallery screamed to heaven for help. Some of the children took boards from the junk pile to use them as bridges to walk on. The old couple who lived upstairs in the schoolhouse was responsible for cleaning and waited forever to wash the outhouse building. I believe none of the teachers knew our problem because they had a bathroom inside the school building that was kept locked. I had my own system when we lived in the refugee camp in Austria when I was pushed out of the long line of refugees in front of the outhouse, and since I had no barn to hide in, used one of the old tall, wide graveyard stones to hide behind. It gave me enough space between it and the wall that surrounded our school, graveyard, church and castle. A large pyramid of stacked firewood was a good place to hide paper if I had need of it. I was sure the Lord understood my problem and the occupant inside this neglected grave dating to the eleventh century was nothing but bones.

THE RAG PRINCESS
WITH A SILVER SPOON

We desperately needed a place for our few belongings. The nice owner of one of the local lumberyards gave Martin some boards he no longer had use for, so he could build a large shelf. He even furnished a hammer and nails to put it together. From now on we did not need to stumble or walk around all the objects we had kept on the floor. It even made enough room for us to eat or do my homework on the old scratched-up folding table Mother had gotten from one of the restaurant's beer gardens. She also had found a few old C-ration crates from the U.S. military to push under the beds with our few pieces of clothing she showed us how to fold nicely.

For the sewing and mending jobs she managed to receive, she needed my help to get all the necessary items. It was a certain color of thread, a sewing needle and a pair of scissors. I started on the third floor, knocked at the door and told the lady that Mother needed it for a sewing job. She did not look very happy about it and said she wanted it returned the next day, handed it to me and slammed the door shut behind me. The problem was, Mother needed more, plus different colors of threads and a scissors, which I had to beg for each day at another door. Soon people no longer opened their doors and I could hear them say, "Oh, it's that refugee girl again," and if they opened the door say, "What is it you need again today?" The tone of their voices and the looks I received haunted me in my dreams at night. I finally sat on the staircase crying because this time it was a cooking pot we needed because ours had a hole that needed to be soldered. We finally had managed to get a little electric cooker with two burners to make our own lunch and dinner. Still sitting there while crying I made myself the promise that one day I would have hundreds of needles and scissors so I could give to the people in need. That must have been when God had seen my tears and sent me an angel in disguise. It was the wife of the doctor, who had moved into the castle. She caught me crying, sat next to me and offered anytime I needed something her door was open for me. With joy I ran upstairs, telling Mother who I met, but forgot all about the pot. The following day I knocked on the doctor's apartment. It felt like heaven when she handed me a cooking pot and told me we could keep it. "And this is for you," she smiled, pointing to a silver spoon inside the pot. She told me it was too big for her two little boys and too small for her. Now I no longer had to eat my soup with a fork and drink the liquid after. Mother was happy for me. Sometimes she joked and called me her little rag princess because we were poor and lived in a castle.

Our forest ranger finally managed to give us some firewood for the winter. Mother did the chopping and Martin stacked the pieces against the back wall of the dugout to dry. It was full of small sheds belonging to the different apartments only we could not have one, because we lived in guest rooms.

Our pastor came for a short visitation, bringing us food from a care package he had received. Mother apologized for sitting in the church balcony each Sunday because we looked like hobos. Smiling, he assured her he did not mind, saying God looked only at our hearts. Now the church was practically next door and not like in Austria where we had to walk one-half day to get to the Lutheran Church, just to arrive as the service was over. I actually enjoyed sitting on the balcony with the late-coming farmers who fell asleep during service, because our pastor was very soft spoken. The only disturbance was mostly the squeaking of pull-out seats, the birds that had nested in the upper unoccupied balcony or if someone's song-book or hat got accidentally pushed overboard and landed in the sanctuary. Before the pastor left, he gave Mother an address of a deaconess in Switzerland who later mailed us a package containing some of their long garments, aprons and snow white bloomers with handmade lace around the upper legs, which Mother turned into beautiful dresses for us using the lace for collars. She was an excellent seamstress, sewing every stitch by hand because while fleeing East Germany we had to leave our treadle sewing machine behind. The 25-watt light bulb we were allowed to use caused a problem for Mother's bad eyesight. It made her become inventive and each night she climbed up on her "throne" as she called it—sitting on a folding chair on top of that wiggly beer garden table to be closer to the light. When she got too tired, she woke one of us up to pull guard duty to make sure she would not tumble down in case she would doze off. The nights it had been my turn, I was extra tired during class the next day and was laughed at when the teacher had to wake me up.

GETTING ADJUSTED

Slowly I began to pick up the strange sounds of the village dialect. Many times I heard them laugh and giggle behind my back as I had problems with some of the pronunciation. Each time I had a chance to be alone, I would practice it talking to myself, but I had to make sure Mother was not listening. She was firmly against the dialect, saying it would interfere with writing. How right she was. I found out in school when a classmate asked me if "budder" was spelled with a hard or soft "d." Since there was no hard or soft letter in our alphabet, I figured it was their invention to help them with speaking the dialect. So they had invented a hard and soft "p" and "b" and "t" and "d." That's when I smiled at my classmate and said you spell butter with two hard "ds."

In needlecraft we got a new teacher. I heard she was a refugee and hoped for a good relationship. My disappointment followed noticing how cold and distant she treated me. Out project was to knit a long scarf. Knitting needles as well as yarn was almost impossible to buy. Since our industry had been destroyed by the war we still lacked so many things, like school books and any kind of paper, soap and detergents, medication or fabric and thread. One could not find it in stores unless he still possessed it from a long time ago. I had retired from my job of door-to-door begging, but we heard that there was a man who could turn the spokes of bicycles into knitting needles. Because we could not pay him with money, he was willing to trade and accepted Mother's offer to mend all his socks and sweaters. Our doctor's wife gave me one of her old sweaters to open up and use the yarn for my school project. In return, I volunteered to untangle several mountains of washed gauze bandages waiting to be untangled and rolled up, so her husband could use them again for his patients.

Most of us second graders had a rough time handling those long ten-inch needles with our small hands. It caused dropped stitches and by getting confused with the beginning and end stitch, we increased or decreased the edges of the scarf. This caused a lot of tears, which our teacher took advantage of. She took home the bad scarves to bring them back corrected. The parents being thankful their daughters made an "A" or "B" sent baskets with butter, eggs, meats and baked goods. The day we received our report cards, I had good grades in every subject except Needlecraft. I was not just disappointed, but I felt hurt looking at that ugly scarf. Mother smiled when I showed her the scarf I had around my neck with wavy edges. She was sure in time with practice I would manage a better grade next year.

Finally winter had arrived. It was a beautiful sight looking down from our window and seeing the village covered with a white snow blanket. Martin had found a job as a clerk at a furniture design company. He had to take the train to the city before I got up in the morning and came home tired in the evening. We finally got some good news about Mother's three sisters who all survived the war by fleeing from the Russians across the Baltic to northern Germany. I had not seen my mother that happy for a long time. Soon letters crossed to each other and I felt sorry for our old mailman who had to climb the stairs to our "two-hole-apartment" as we had named it, delivering mail filled with love, hugs and tears of joy.

OUR FIRST CHRISTMAS

When Mother woke me up for school, telling me it had snowed, I rushed to the window to see how much. To see everything in white made me homesick. I remembered the snow castle my brothers had made and the snowman guarding the entrance, wearing a steel helmet and holding a stick as a weapon. Our little house now belonged to a Polish family. Hopefully they had children who enjoyed my yard long skis, my sled and all my dolls. Too bad we could not write to them to tell them to open up the floorboards in the attic to find all the treasures we had hidden until we returned, because our village now had a new Polish name. For unknown reasons our school closed early that day. Throwing their backpacks into the snow the girls got into a big snowball fight with the boys. Because I had no hat and mittens I rushed home to watch the rest of the battle from my window.

In the afternoon we girls had our needlecraft lesson while the Catholic students had religion. To have a little entertainment while stitching snowflakes and bells on a piece of fabric, our teacher handed me a book with a long Christmas story to read. I was wondering why she had chosen me. Maybe she knew I was the best in reading and writing or maybe she wanted to keep me occupied before she left the classroom. To have more light I took the book to the window where I could see her standing in the schoolyard flirting with the new priest.

A few days later our school planned to have the annual Christmas celebration. Our teacher chose some of the students to take part in the large nativity play, some to sing in the choir and others to read Christmas-related poems. My friend Kathy and I had a small skit.

Finally it was time for our Christmas play. It took place in the very same restaurant whose dance hall had been our temporary shelter when we arrived as refugees from Austria. Filled with folding chairs, it was beautifully decorated with lights and a large Christmas tree. To rehearse our skit once more, Kathy and I met behind the stage curtain. She had brought a large box with a fox stole she had talked her grandmother into letting us use for this occasion. First came Christmas songs presented by the upper grades, next the nativity play with students from different classes. Some of my classmates wore their white flannel nightgowns and a wreath in their unbraided long hair as angels. Joseph seemed to be upset because he constantly had to hold up his beard while Mary, his spouse, was welcoming the three Kings and the shepherds, who knelt in front of her large diapered doll that was placed in a crib filled with straw. All the girls were jealous of Hanna who played Mary because she had such an important part.

Hedwig, a girl from third grade was next to recite the Christmas story from the Bible. The teacher had chosen her because she did not speak very fast but loud. Standing in front of such a big audience caused her to shake and stutter. We all felt sorry for her. But when Hedwig began to use one arm rotating it constantly on the side of her dress as if she was turning a big wheel, the entire audience started to laugh. The louder they laughed, the faster she turned her wheel, that's when we could no longer keep from laughing until we had tears in our eyes.

It was time for our skit. Kathy and I dragged the large box into the middle of the stage and while the curtain slowly opened, we were still giggling about Hedwig's performance, who was now crying in the back. First Kathy spoke how war had caused so much poverty and problems. I pointed at the large box, a package I had received from my aunt in America as a help in a time of trouble. Bending down I opened the box to show her the precious gift I had received by pulling out the old fox to hang around my neck. That's when the strong fumes of the mothballs hit me and made an end to the beauty of it. An attack of sneezing prevented me from talking. Instead of wrapping it around my neck, I threw it over to Kathy, who caught it and started coughing. And when the audience laughed and whistled, we made an end to our wonderful presentation, threw the fox back into the box and kicked it to the back of the stage were Hedwig laughed with the rest of our theater group.

At the end of the evening the U.S. military handed out gifts for the great performers and for poverty-struck children. Before the soldier who scratched my name off the list handed me the ribbon wrapped gift he asked someone to translate something. He asked me if I rather prefer to have the fox, which made us laugh. I shook my head and grabbed my gift. It was a beautiful warm hat, a long scarf and a pair of mittens—just what I needed for this cold weather. A second gift was a game of checkers. Later on my way home I felt warm and happy and I wondered how different people were. Our neighbors who had plenty did not seem to care much, but people far away across the ocean gave me what I needed to keep warm. Looking up to the stars I was sure that I would always remember this Christmas.

THE BLACK SHEEP

It was New Year's night. Martin, who returned from getting firewood, said that people were gathered in the school and churchyard. We got dressed to go to see what it was all about. Everyone was standing around and visiting as if they were waiting for something. One of the children mentioned they were waiting for the Pastor to hold a speech. A few minutes later he stood in his doorway and spoke a few words. He prayed thanking God for carrying us through the year that was now passed and to give us wisdom, guidance and His protection for the coming year. After that we all sang the song "Let Us All Thank God With Our Hearts, Lips and Hands." It was a song, which most of us knew by heart. During the last verse the steeple clock stroked a loud twelve and the bells began to ring. In this crisp and clear winter night I could hear bells from faraway churches ringing in the New Year. With a smile and a warm handshake people wished each other a very "happy and blessed New Year." This was the moment when some of the boys lit their firecrackers that jumped around like frogs and made everyone take off in different directions. We took off to get on the bridge behind the iron gate leading to the castle. At home I opened the window and listened to all the bells near and far, enjoying the wonderful sound of peace in the cold air of this winter night.

After Christmas vacation we had a lot of children in school with throat infections that turned into a regular pandemic. I went to visit some of my sick classmates at home who could hardly talk or swallow. I felt so bad being the only one left not being affected by this that I wore my pretty Christmas scarf around my neck, pretending to be sick just out of pure sympathy.

Mother was still sewing and mending for people who paid her with food instead of money. One day our landlady informed Mom it was time to pay rent. Mother, who was not able to come up with the full amount, asked her if she could work it off by helping in the kitchen or doing a sewing job. But her request was denied. Ever since Austria I had not seen my mother cry like this time. She lacked ten Dmarks to pay the rent. To be of help to her, I came up with the idea to take it out of the offering plate next Sunday. She could not believe her eyes, hugged me and thanked the Lord when I told her I had found it in the sand of the churchyard. But like they say "Lies have short legs," I found out how short when we were called to see the Pastor the following day. Mother hoped it was about a new care package, but I knew someone must have watched and reported my wrong doing.

Mother and I were asked to take a seat in the Pastor's study. Her face was so happy when he shook her hand while he apologized for what he had to tell her. I looked away, knowing what it was. Mother could not believe what she heard. Now it was my turn to tell the truth. I knew lying was a sin, but so was stealing. The Lord knew I was already guilty but I believed He still loved me because I wanted to help and not hurt my mother. So I kept insisting I had found the money in the sand. I knew that after each wedding the bride, before leaving the church, would stand in the doorway and open her little satin pouch she carried tied to her large flower bouquet and threw money into the gathered crowd. It was mostly us children picking it up, but after everyone had gone we searched for some time in case we missed some coins still lying in the sand. No one would believe she threw paper money. Now I was sitting there, and to spare my mother pain and embarrassment, insisted on being innocent, knowing I had become the black sheep of the Pastor's flock. My great idea to help my mother now had turned into a regular nightmare. After an hour had passed, the Pastor gave up for the day but told me to return each night until I would tell the truth.

Two more evenings he wasted his time with pleading and praying. Now it was the fourth night. I was supposed to pray that the Holy Spirit would give me the courage to confess. Politely I bended my head and folded my hands. I prayed silently for God to please get this Pastor off my back, otherwise this could go on for the next few years. I believed God still loved me and how sorry I was for taking this money that actually belonged to Him. He probably did not mind as much as the Pastor, because He owned heaven and earth plus the entire universe. After I had finished my silent prayer I looked at Mother who was still praying. I felt sorry for her having a daughter like me, she who did not have one rebellious bone in her body, when she was facing a higher authority connected to God.

My eyes caught the beautiful picture hanging on the wall behind the desk. I had seen this picture of Jesus as the Good Shepherd holding a little lamb many times in books, but I never wondered why He held it so close to His heart. Maybe it had left the right path like I did. This kind of pity and compassion that Jesus had I needed now in the form of a few kind words, forgivingness and the promise that Mother could keep the money she needed. It would have broken the dam holding back my tears and my confession. But without any sign of mercy and understanding, I just sat there swallowing my tears and tightening my lips.

While the Pastor cleared his throat several times and rubbed his delicate white hands together still waiting for the truth, I wondered if he really knew what "truth" was all about. He, who sat in velvet covered chairs in a squeaky clean study in his ten-room house, reading and preaching the scriptures, did not know how blessed he was. Maybe someone should tell him about our lives. A few years ago we were forced to leave our home to live in a refugee camp in Austria until the war was over. We had to endure being cold, lice and bed ticks and beg for our food, living together with seven families in one room and calling two bunk beds our home. Each time we turned our backs, they would steal our belongings. After the war we came to this village with just a few clothes and depending on the mercy and handouts of others, stripped of all pride and dignity. I came so close to screaming this kind of truth into his face, but being well raised and in the presence of my mother, I kept silent.

All he had to do was take off his blinders and look at us. My mother was a picture of devastation but not the kind he could hang on his wall for decoration. There was that terrible long scar across the top of one hand. The hatchet had slipped while chopping firewood by moonlight because during daytime she worked for food. The reason why she wore her dresses longer was to hide her legs with those dark spots showing severe malnutrition—caused by giving us her portion of food saying she was not hungry or she already had eaten. Her shoelaces were ugly paper strings we took off my aunt Lena's Christmas package.

Finally the Pastor's wife opened the door, telling him it was high time for dinner. The steeple clock hammered a loud nine. He took off his glasses and leaned back in his chair looking at the ceiling as if he was waiting for a word from God. Maybe he had given up on me and given me to God, because suddenly he jumped up telling me with a tender voice and smile I was excused. Wondering about this situation I asked him if he wanted us to come back the following night. "Only if you are ready to tell the truth," he answered, smiling again.

While Mother was still talking to him, I managed to weasel out of the door while whispering "goodnight." I sat on the steps in front of the house, and while I was waiting for my mother, felt free as a bird out of its cage.

That evening while Mother prayed with me, she paused just a second after she had said "and lead us not into temptation." Then when she hugged me and told me she loved me, I began to cry. She did not have to say anything, but when she held me I sensed she had known the truth all along.

FINDING FATHER
AND MOTHER'S NEW JOB

For Father's Day our teacher came up with the idea of students to rise and honor their fathers by saying what had happened to them. Died in Tobruk; missing in the African desert; died at sea; killed in Norway; imprisoned in Russia were the answers, scattered all over the world. Only a few classmates' fathers had returned from the war. Our family was still searching for our dad.

One day Mother returned from the Red Cross with good news. They finally had made connection with my father who lived in the north of Germany, still being occupied by the British. In his first letter we got through the mail he asked Mother to be patient, it could take a long time for him to be able to travel. He was afraid to be captured by the Americans because all he had to wear was his uniform. Mother could not see this as a problem and wrote in her answer to get a shirt and pair of pants at the Red Cross or borrow them from someone to return later. It did not have to be anything new, because after the war we all looked like hobos. When Father came up with more excuses, Mother became suspicious but we lacked money to travel to find out what his real reason was.

Our pastor had finally found a job for Mom. A small farm needed a farmhand for sunny days and a seamstress on rainy days. Mother was happy even though they could only pay with food. After school I went to see her and got a big piece of bread with homemade butter and an apple. Their oldest son George, who had been wounded in battle and wore a glass eye, was very friendly and took me along to their plum orchard. I could not believe my eyes. While he picked plums of all colors and shapes he asked me to fill up the long baskets with red, black and white berries that grew between the long rows of trees. I asked him if I could eat some of those miniature grapes. He laughed saying those were called currants and I could eat all I wanted. The trees provided shade and after I had filled up all the baskets and eaten red and white currants, George, who noticed my bleeding lips, took me to a nearby spring. The ice cold water felt good. He apologized for not warning me about the acid of sour fruits. Sitting on the wagon, taking home all the wonderful harvest, I was sure that someday I would grow my very own paradise of fruits and berries.

Our class had a new teacher. Though he was not an old man, he had lost a lot of his hair. The rest he wore as a half circle short cut from side to side. He was stout, quiet and friendly and when he smiled his eyes would smile at the same time. He loved children, art and music. Almost every few days we learned a new folk song. Sometimes he selected a group to stand in front of the class to sing. Standing there side by side, facing our class and the teacher, I noticed being pushed to the right. I finally had to push the girl on my right side, which happened several times. Because we were singing, I could not ask what was happening. After the song had ended I no longer had to wonder. Returning to our seats I could see a water puddle on the floor where we had been standing. Now everyone could see what had happened and the entire class started to laugh until the teacher called for silence. All he said was that an accident is nothing to laugh about and if he sees one more grinning face he will order him or her to clean it up.

One day I had to stay after class because I had called one of the girls "a stupid cow." It was Mary who had thick pigtails long enough to sit on. Each of our seats had a small inkpot in the desk to dip our feather pens we wrote with. Getting up and playing around, she smeared my writing with one of her braids, which always smelled like her cow stable. Being upset, I called her a stupid cow, which I had been called many times by the village children. Crying, she ran to the teacher to complain about it. I could tell how happy she was hoping I would get the usual punishment, the stick across the open hand. Some students got it more than once, especially after making the teacher mad by making a fist at the last moment. After everyone had gone I only got a lecture on how to be nice to my classmates in the future. In addition I had to write a report about "The difference between cows and people." Writing was one of my favorite subjects and I had plenty time to think about it. The next day I had to turn it in.

> Cows have spots, we only have moles and freckles. They eat grass until we eat them. They have four legs to stand on and we have only two. Calves stand on their legs right after birth, while humans crawl around on the ground until they finally realize they have two legs to stand on. We can speak and tell them what to do, all they can say is moo. They have to pull wagons and labor for us, while we whip them to do so. We can use our toilet while sitting down, but cows spread their nature call all over the street while standing up. We can wash to keep clean but cows have to wait until it rains. When they get a chance to eat, they eat a double portion and bring it up later to chew it again. When we try to do the same, we can eat a lot and bring it up, too, but we are not able to chew it again. Cows have extremely big eyes and never need glasses like we do, because they do not have to strain them by reading and writing like we do. Cows are very stubborn animals and if we are stubborn, we are called "bull headed." They never mind if we call them stupid. But if we call someone a "stupid cow" we have to write a report about it.

The following day at school I handed it to the teacher who after reading it grinned and said he would put it into his collection, whatever that meant.

Sitting in the classroom.

AMERICA'S GIFT—"QUAKER FOOD"

Things began to change. America had decided to help German schoolchildren with Quaker food. In my class it was Hans, Emma and I who received a nice metal container with a snap-on lid for these lunches. It made us happy but the rest of our classmates jealous. Since the castle was right next to the school, the owner had volunteered to prepare and serve it. While handing out the food our landlady put on her friendly face like a mask only I could see through. That was during recess, when we stood in line with all the pupils from other classes. She would turn to block my view so I never found out if I got a full dipper like she gave everyone else. To me it did not really matter, since I never ate her watered-down food. The cocoa had hardly any chocolate flavor left and the rest had a lack of taste. It made me wonder if she planned on using the good amount of leftovers to doctor up for her many restaurant guests. My sister always ate her Quaker lunch but I had come up with a much better idea. To cure the jealousy of my classmates I traded it for fantastic sandwiches, which my classmates' mothers prepared for me the following day. Though I hated to see it being wrapped in ugly newspaper, I rather ate some of the print rather than receiving it from the hands of my classmates with dark brown colored, outhouse fingernails. But for my landlady I always had a nice, polite "thank you" each time she handed me my Quaker lunch while thinking if she only knew my secret, she would be so mad and stomp herself into the ground like the nasty little dwarf in the fairy tale *Rumpelstilzkin*.

After school Elisabeth and I went to the farm to help Mother pick up the fallen apples and pears from a lot of trees growing in the backyard. This place was a large, steep downhill meadow with grass up to our knees. It was not an easy job until I realized that a lot of fruit had rolled down the hill and piled up along the fence. We filled up many baskets that we lined up in the large hallway of the farmhouse. While it was still daylight, we each took a rake and left for one of their fields to turn over the hay. Sweaty and tired we returned, resting on the bench in front of the house, while the farmer's wife fixed us our dinner to take home. Before we left, the farmer ordered his wife to unwrap our dinner to see what she had given us. When he saw the large hunk of plain bread, he chased his wife into the kitchen to add a large portion of smoked meat to it, while he promised her a beating if she ever tried it again. Though Mother tried to calm him down by saying it was not necessary to have meat each time, he insisted that we had earned it. From the neighbors we knew that after each time he drank too much, he would beat her. Somehow we felt sorry for her. But each time it came to giving, he was better than her. Mother, who was suspicious of the large fruit basket we had received to take home, asked us to pick out the damaged or spoiled apples and pears. We could not believe what she had done. Only the top layer of fruits were excellent, the rest of them looked bad. All three of us sat that night and cut, salvaging what we could.

Our Quaker lunches lasted for over one year. After my sandwich paradise had closed I needed to come up with a new idea. Because many of the children had problems with writing and drawing, I began to trade my work for food. Late afternoons I played ball with the son of the doctor who was a few years younger than I, or I took his little brother in his stroller to the graveyard outside the village and watered the family grave. We used to rest in the shade on one of the benches under a large shade tree and before we left this place of silence, I pulled out the weeds growing on graves of unknown soldiers that were identified with a steel helmet over a wooden cross. Coming home, I was invited for dinner at the large table to enjoy a good meal with the doctor and his family.

MOVIE TIME

Through his job Martin had found some friends his own age who lived mostly out of town. He used his weekends to spend time with them and to get a good meal. A farmer in our neighborhood had volunteered, while in church, to invite a refugee for lunch each Sunday after the service. Since their daughter was one year older than my sister, they chose Elisabeth. Because Mother did not have to work on the farm on Sunday, she took me blueberry picking. We could not buy canning glasses, so we used old beer bottles we found and cleaned. Sometimes we would find some mushrooms for our evening meal.

Each time we noticed a blown-up bladder of an animal hanging in front of a farm it was a sign that they had butchered. That gave everyone a chance to get some butcher broth. Some farmers canned their own meat and cooked their sausages in casings in a super large enamel tub. When casings busted some of the sausage cooked into the broth and Mother used it to make a soup to die for.

Finally our village opened up a movie theater. Metzger restaurant sacrificed their upstairs dance room once a week for movie time. At a certain time of the day it was entrance free for children. I begged Mother to let me go, who after checking out the display pictures, gave her permission.

My first movie was "Tarzan." It was an experience I would always remember. On my way home I made a quick stop at the doctor's apartment, because I had promised their housemaid I would tell her about it. She was thirteen, as old as my sister, and worked until late in the evening. I found her with her arms buried in the dishwater and happy I had kept my promise. Tarzan's jungle was a strange place for us Germans and soon she was listening, staring at me while resting her hands in the dishwater. She did not pay any attention to the grandmother entering the kitchen to get busy peeling and cutting up vegetables. While she was listening, she held on to her knife without paying attention to her job, smiling about cheetah, Tarzan's monkey, and enjoying my retelling. When I pictured how the jungle had caught on fire, the doctor's wife came in to get some of the bandages we had rolled up and more supplies for her husband. Standing and listening, she finally pulled out a chair from the table to sit imagining the jungle burn, while Tarzan and Jane on top of an elephant were guiding the animals to safety and their monkey swinging from tree to tree, following them. While the whole kitchen was on fire, the door opened again. Only this time it was the doctor himself who had been waiting for his wife to return, causing my jungle to disappear and bringing reality back. His wife apologized, the maid renewed her cold dishwater, the grandmother kept cutting her vegetables and I managed to squeeze next to the doctor out of the door while feeling somewhat guilty.

While climbing upstairs to our "hole in the wall" apartment, I could not keep from smiling, noticing how I had been able to manage to turn a kitchen into a jungle.

I enjoyed the times I had a chance to go see a movie. Only when the weather became cold and we moved our folding chairs close to the black iron potbelly stove, we had to watch the movie through clouds of smoke until our eyes burned and we looked like we cried instead of laughing at a funny picture.

Going home and passing by the doctor's apartment, I felt sorry for the young housemaid so I snuck in and made sure the air was clean to entertain her with the new movie I had seen, leaving the kitchen door ajar. From there I watched the long hallway to see if someone came. That's when I used the excuse to visit their bathroom. It was a large room, built over the restaurant with a modern flushable stool. The shiny white bathtub was only something for me to dream about. Because this room was the coolest in the apartment, it was also used as a pantry. The ruffled curtains hanging on the long shelf against the wall were hiding a forbidden paradise of snacks. Butter, lunchmeats, cheeses and other milk products, jams and glasses full of things I never tasted were very tempting. I usually satisfied myself with one of the sour pickles out of the large jar. By the time I flushed the stool I was finished eating it. Only once I was caught with my mouth full leaving the bathroom. Thank God it was only one of the doctor's patients going home. From that time on I made sure this would not happen again.

THE STEW AND MY SISTER'S
FIRST JOB

E lisabeth was now thirteen and finished with school. Our pastor had found a wonderful couple who was looking for a housemaid. He was the principal in a nearby village living with his sick wife in the large schoolhouse. I almost cried while seeing her standing, smiling and waving on the train's platform holding her little suitcase.

After class I missed her walking with me to see Mother at the farm, while remembering all the good and bad times we had together. I found Mother sewing in the storeroom where the sewing machine was placed in front of a window. I dropped off my backpack and went into the kitchen to see what was cooking that smelled so delicious. The kitchen was a very dark place with only one window facing the inside of the cow stable, which had been built onto the house. Each time someone opened the door to walk into the house, a swarm of flies would follow. The second evil was the stable odor spreading throughout the rooms. I looked into the large kettle standing on the stove. The top had a layer of bacon bits. Though the farmer's wife lacked on many things, I had to admit, she was a great cook making everything tasty. I ran back to Mother to report the good news. Being hungry, I could hardly wait to eat and helped set the table in the large living room. With the farmer and George we were five people. After we all were seated and George had cut the bread, his mother carried in the large kettle holding the soup dipper in the other hand. I hoped she would not stir the bacon down, so I could get a lot of it. It was one of my favorite meats.

The sunlight shining through the large windows helped me to view the dark top crust better than I could in the dark kitchen. For a moment I could not believe my eyes. Some of the pieces had wings trying to fly out of the hot liquid. What I thought was bacon, had been nothing else but flies! I watched the soup dipper pushing down the crusted mess and being distributed throughout the stew drowning the still alive insects. Helpless I stared at Mother who I could tell was aware of this situation. Her eyes, as well as the expression on her face, spoke louder than words. Now I knew the reason why the many curly glue strips hanging down everywhere from the ceiling did not catch many flies. They were all in the food and I had eaten them without being aware of it. I did not want my mother to lose her job. Picking up my spoon I viewed the wonderful smelling stew on my plate being tempted to try and fish out the dead flies. Everyone was eating as if nothing was wrong. Looking down I closed my eyes, thought about all the good-tasting currants and plums and George in the orchard who had been kind to me, allowing me to eat as much as I wanted and ate until my plate was empty. Before anyone could ask me if I wanted seconds, I took my plate and hurried to the kitchen, filled the sink with dishwater and waited for my mother.

Sunday after church I went to see my sister. Walking for over one hour, I took shortcuts by crossing fields and meadows until I came to a wide deep creek. A small wooden area surrounded the bridge crossing the water. Though it was a nice sunny day this area was dark and spooky to walk through. Arriving in the village, it did not take very long to find the large schoolhouse in which the principal and his wife lived. I spotted Elisabeth in the large fenced-in backyard. She was so happy to see me and cried. While pulling weeds in the vegetable beds, she poured out her heart telling me how difficult life had become for her. I listened how she had to get up early, prepare meals and clean, do the laundry once a week, polish the wooden floors and drag out the large area rug and hang it up to beat it. She had to chop the firewood and work in the garden. She had to keep the classrooms clean and on weekends wash the floors and staircase up to the fourth floor. Because the principal's wife distrusted and refused to sleep with him, Elisabeth had to share the large bed with her, while the principal spent his nights in the maid room upstairs. The only privacy she had was in the yard or if she was allowed to take a walk. She finally took me inside to introduce me to the friendly couple who allowed her to take a few hours off and show me the village. We stopped at a nearby pond, sat in the grass and talked. Feeling sorry for her I talked a lot about school and Mother to cheer her up. On our way back I had to promise not to say anything to Mom that might make her worry.

When I left, the sun was setting. I knew I had to hurry to make it home before dark. The wooden area by the creek looked dark and spooky. In vain I tried to find another crossing. I also knew that the longer I waited to enter the darkness, the more my fear would elevate. With the little courage I had left I said a short prayer and charged like a bull running without looking right or left until I was across the bridge and out on the other side. Looking back to see if anyone had followed me I took a deep breath. Since the sun was down I skipped my shortcuts and took the main road through the next village. I finally made it home just before dark, so Mother did not have to worry about me any longer.

THE WEDDING AND THE SEVEN-ROOM APARTMENT

I heard music, then sounds of a marching band coming closer and closer. Looking down from our west window I could see the band coming around the corner, followed by an empty wagon pulled by horses with heads and tails full of flowers. Happy village children hopped and skipped behind this little parade. I ran downstairs and lined up with the children to see what would happen next. We all ended up in a nearby one-way street and stopped at the last house. The farmer's daughter was going to have a wedding. Standing in the front yard she served beer and sandwiches to the band members and jam-filled doughnuts to us children, while she watched some of the men load her grandmother's furniture, which she had inherited, carefully onto the wagon. The last two items were her large hope chest and a beautiful white baby cradle.

From there we followed this happy parade to the lumberyard, where the owner had given Martin the boards for our kitchen shelf. The band members and others were given more beer, plus cream and jam-filled doughnuts while the wagon was being unloaded. After I ate my second doughnut, I carried the others back home inside my apron.

The following week was the big wedding. I belonged to the little girl choir—singing for funerals, baptisms and weddings. Standing on the first balcony of the church close to the large organ, we started to sing the wedding song, "Take My Hand and Lead Me" as soon as the wedding parade entered the church. Little girls in long white dresses were leading spreading flowers across the carpet from the baskets each carried for the bride and groom to walk on. Behind them followed a little boy, holding the pillow with the wedding bands and behind him came the bride and groom. The little evergreen wreathes that were stitched onto the bottom of her beautiful gown of satin and lace, were a sign of virginity. The couple walked arm in arm slowly toward the church's altar where the Pastor was waiting. In her other arm she held a large bouquet of red roses. The length of her veil, measured according to the wealth of both families, was being held on both sides and back by children to keep it off the ground. The couple was followed by family members, relatives, friends and other guests in sets of two. The length of the parade was based on the importance or wealth of the wedding couple. Kissing each other at the end of the ceremony was against the rules of the church.

On the way out the couple stopped in the church's doorway. Village children had gathered, waiting for the bride to empty her coin-filled satin pouch she carried. After she threw all the coins to the right and to the left, kids went wild picking them up, creating enough space for the wedding parade on the way home. We children searched for coins in front of the church a long time after each wedding. I usually found some in the climbing green ivy and between the flowers on top of the old graves, while others found theirs still hiding in the sandy road.

By the time the wedding parade arrived at the sawmill's mansion, someone was awaiting the couple in front of the door, holding a tray with two small glasses filled equally with liqueur. The bride and groom were to start drinking at the same time and the one who emptied the glass first became the head of the family. In this case, both emptied their glass at the same time.

It was an old tradition that during the wedding night the bride was to be abducted. The groom, accompanied by several friends, began his search. The bridemaids would take her to a secret hideout. A lot of conspiracy and blackmail was used to find her that sometimes lasted until the following day. To find an answer for this crazy tradition I came up with my own idea. Because of all the night dancing and heavy drinking going on, it may have prevented the groom to father his firstborn in such a drunken state. Some of these wedding celebrations lasted for several days.

In our little church choir I had a girl standing next to me named Linda. She was one year younger and also a refugee. She thought living in the castle was like heaven on earth. Telling her all about it I had to disappoint her. Her family had found shelter in a large mansion across from the town's train station. When she told me about the 7 rooms they had, I was sure she was making up a story. After she invited me to see her three-bedroom, living room with kitchen, study and playroom apartment, I asked Mother if I could go. Being a little suspicious, she insisted on coming along to meet her parents. The evening of our visit we ran into a big surprise. The landlord had allowed Linda's family to use the attic that stretched over the entire mansion. Sheets and blankets draped over clothes lines divided the rooms. I counted 8 rooms along with the bathroom. It faced north and south, creating a large wide walkway space in the middle. Linda's parents took Mother to their living room and she lifted each sheet to show me the rest of her fancy apartment. I was amazed to see how they used the walls for hanging things, bricks for elevating and boards for flat surfaces. This family was extremely creative and Mother and I talked about it a long time after our visit.

GOOD AND BAD NEWS

For almost one year Mother had tried to inspire Father to come home. One day he surprised all of us by knocking on our door. It was a great joy! He appeared different to me than I expected in civilian clothes, since I only remembered him in uniform. When he asked about Elisabeth, Martin offered to take him to see her. He seemed pleased and surprised how much we had grown and changed. I had not seen him for over five years and did not know what to say and since Mother and he had a lot to talk about, I went to play ball with Otto, the doctor's son.

Father's profession was an upholsterer. He could make great looking couches and chairs, mattresses and other beautiful things. A few days later Mother told him that the farm she worked at would allow him some space in their large barn to start a business. He backed out with a million excuses, which made Mother not just sad, but also suspicious. Her distrust rose when he did not want to wait for the mailman and went to the post office to get the mail. His excuse for that was that he had no job and needed to walk.

One day the lady who lived on the third floor came to see Mother. She had something important to show her that flew out of her toilet. Most of the castle still had the old sewer system dating back to the year 1313. It was a very large round pipe starting at the sewer and ending at the castle's roof, sticking out a piece. The toilets on each floor were slanted smaller side pipes with a wooden lid. During windy weather we used a bucket filled with water to carefully lift the lid to sink the papers people had used, which were flying around in the main pipe trying to escape. When the lady opened her toilet lid, a letter flew out that had been written to my father. Cleaning it the best she could, it was bad news. Now we knew why Father had taken a whole year to come home. A woman he had lived with had been expecting his child. Both hoped that her husband, who was getting a discharge from a POW camp, would make it home in time to become the father. It turned out he came much later than expected and divorced his unfaithful wife.

I had never seen my father so angry when he was told how his secret came at last to the surface. Each evening after I went to bed I could hear my parents argue until late at night. Mother was right when she told him he only married her to take care of his four children left behind after their mother died. Sometimes it looked like he was ready to physically attack her by raising his arm. But when he looked at me, he came to his senses.

It was not long until he moved into the storeroom on the same floor after the landlord had emptied it for him. Martin, his pride and joy from his first marriage, moved in with him. Later, Father found a job at the same place my brother worked. Each time I played outside and saw them walking home from the train, I found a hiding place until they passed by. Mother was asked to come to the divorce court where Father used Martin to testify she had been unfaithful to him while he was away in the military. When Martin was nervous he would stutter and changed his story each time—the court did not believe it. Mother left the divorce up to the court and they decided the marriage could continue, if both parties were willing to. From that day on Father hated Mother and said he would do so until he died for not giving him his freedom. He refused to pay child support by constantly changing jobs. Each time the government got ready to deduct the support from his paycheck he quit and looked for another job. After he found the lady he had fathered another child with, who was one year younger than I, Father moved with my brother to the Black Forest where she lived with her son.

Mother had found a job in the next village's paper factory. The young maid in the castle had left and was replaced with an older girl who was less friendly. I used to hear the maid's prayers through the wall. Now there was nothing but silence. Life on the fourth floor had become lonely and spooky. I spent a lot of time alone in the woods picking berries or looking for mushrooms. On rainy days I would visit a classmate or go to see if I could be of some help in the doctor's apartment. On weekends I would go to see Elisabeth. Life for me had drastically changed.

PICKING BLUEBERRIES WITH BETTY

Betty was one of my classmates. She asked me one day if I would take her along to pick berries. Actually, I did not like the idea, but to have some company I finally agreed.

It was a sunny afternoon when we found us a good picking spot in the woods. The place seemed to be still untouched and had large bushes full of blueberries. We placed our buckets next to a large tree and used our smaller containers for picking. Betty's was so small that it caused her valuable time to run and empty it. Her happiness about coming along lasted only until she was hungry. When I asked her why she did not bring something to eat, her excuse was that she had no idea picking a few berries would make someone so hungry. Telling her it was not time to eat yet caused her to eat what she picked until her lips were blue. That's when I finally split my sandwich with her, hoping it would make her happy. But I guessed wrong. While she kept picking on the same bush with me, complaining about mosquitoes and backaches, I finally suggested for her to go home. When she insisted that I go along because she was afraid to walk home by herself, I told her to wait until I filled my bucket. Her next complaint was that my container showed more berries than hers. From that time on I kept my bucket close by where I could see it, saying it would save me making long trips. I was upset with myself for taking her along, but feeling sorry for her I helped to fill up hers at the end. By then it was close to sundown and time to leave the forest.

We took the main street and met more people on their way home. When Betty kept complaining how thirsty she was, blaming me for not taking any water along, I told her about the nice cold spring just off the road. I only had used it once or twice while picking berries with my sister. It was located between a large deep crater caused by a war bomb and a newly planted pine tree addition. A narrow trail led to the spring. Betty insisted on going. After we entered the pine tree section, the pathway was so narrow we had to walk behind each other. The fading daylight and not being able to see anything between the side by side planted trees, created a spooky feeling. The only thing we heard was our own footsteps on the moist trail until we came to the spring. We filled our empty picking containers with the cold spring water and rested on the nearby bench talking and laughing, when suddenly I heard a noise. I grabbed Betty's arm and whispered to her to be quiet. For the next few minutes we just listened. Believing I had been mistaken, we continued with our conversation until we both heard the same noise. It sounded as if someone was walking on the same trail we had used. When Betty mentioned it could be a deer coming to the spring, I heard the noise again but as soon as she stopped talking, who or whatever it was, also stopped.

I had been in the woods since I was little while sitting in my stroller. Mother used to push me into a clearing with bright sunlight, while she walked away to pick raspberries on very high bushes reaching into the trees. When I felt uneasy because I could not see her anymore, I would call and she always answered. I learned that if animals hear humans they are silent because they sense danger. But as soon as humans are silent, animals feel safe again and roam around. This was not an animal. It was someone who did not want us to hear him. He only walked when we talked. Our only way out was the large crater on the other side. In all these years after the war it had grown full of trees and underbrush resembling wilderness. It only took us seconds to decide what to do. Grabbing our buckets we ran panic stricken down into the large crater. I found a large stick I used to keep the thorny branches of large blackberry bushes away and tried to stomp them to the ground so Betty could follow me. When I noticed she stopped to pick up some of the berries she had spilled, I told her not to bother because the grass was too high. Fear caused my heart to beat overtime. We found a lot of mud and holes on the bottom until we finally made it to the other side, working ourselves uphill toward the street. There we lined up behind people pushing their loaded bicycles, feeling safe while looking back behind us. I felt relieved no one had followed us.

Nearing the village, Betty began to complain again how her mother would be upset with her for using one whole afternoon for just a handful of berries. I knew what she was after. Acting like I did not know, I told her to look in the mirror when she got home to see how blue her lips and tongue were.

Before we went our separate ways in front of the castle, I made her happy and gave her a lot of my berries. Somehow I felt sorry for her being a spoiled child always sheltered and babied. She probably never had a bad day in her life and could not help the way she was. There was a great difference between the two of us.

The following day Betty had a lot to tell our classmates. She was the big hero who rescued me, leading me through the crater to safety. She pulled up her sleeves to show them all the scratches on her arms as well as her legs, while avoiding looking at me.

Poor Betty, I thought. She made such a big story out of one single experience. In the castle I had to face fear every day and night and never talked about it. I did not try to get the sympathy of my classmates, but I had God watching over me as well as my mother's prayers.

BLACK CHERRY REVENGE

Sometimes Mother would keep our door open for awhile, so I could see the staircase. Each time she placed a new bulb into the ceiling light in the dark hallway our landlady removed it. When I woke up in the morning, Mother had already gone to work on the farm. It was time to go to school. After I had locked the door behind me, I counted my steps while stretching out my hand in the darkness to feel the banister. On the next floor I stretched out my hand again, but before I reached the banister I had lost the floor under my feet and fell down the staircase, landing on the stone tiles of the large hallway of the second floor, right in front of the dragon lady's bedroom door. My metal container for Quaker food had caused a loud noise echoing through this sandstone palace. I had fallen down that very same staircase several times before, but never felt as hurt as this time. Feeling the cold stone floor under me, I hoped someone would come and help me up. After I heard the sound of a door opening, someone was bending over me. It was the dragon staring in my face. One would think that even a dragon would have a heart, but this one didn't. She had placed both hands on her hips, like she needed to hold them up, and stuck her large ugly tongue out at me like nasty children do. Not paying attention to what she said, I rose slowly to my feet, gathered my belongings and made it down to the first floor. My pride was bigger than my pain until I was outside. For a few minutes I stood in the house corner next to the back door, leaning against the wall and cried to relieve the pain I felt physically and mentally, knowing how much she disliked me.

A few days later the doctor's family had their washday. The castle's entire backyard had been used to hang up their laundry. The

163

two trees behind all those sheets and blankets were full of large, but still green plums. This was a great opportunity to pay back the landlady. She was known to make the best plum preserve in the village. In the dugout I found a perfect long stick, which helped attack both trees as high as I could reach. Plums and leaves were flying around to teach the dragon a good lesson.

The following school day our teacher announced that each of us had to bring in an old empty can. Our country had a new enemy—nasty potato bugs had invaded our fields. Until a pesticide was developed, we schoolchildren would have to control this evil. Twice a week we had to search the potato fields to find the bugs and their eggs and burn them in our little metal containers.

It was after school when we left for our battlefields to wipe out the invaders in groups of two per field. Because the cherry trees were loaded with fruit, I had already chosen a certain place for my classmate Emma and me. Mother and I had passed it the year before, on our way to the forest. We saw the farmer standing on his ladder picking cherries, while an old lady who was holding a shopping bag, asked him to sell her a few pounds. By her poor clothing and her accent, one could tell she was a refugee. After he refused she began to plead, which made the farmer mad. To melt his cold heart she knelt on the ground pleading while she was weeping. That's when he told her to leave or he would call his dog to do it.

His trees were planted between the long rows of potatoes with branches loaded heavy with large black cherries hanging low, almost touching the ground. Now we helped him to get rid of his bugs. My plan was, while working, to eat all the cherries we possibly could hold. Emma hesitated because she had to report every wrong thing to her priest. But telling her it would take some weight off the branches to keep them from breaking and we were helping the farmer by saving his potato harvest, she finally agreed. Both of us, being refugees and hungry after school, ate as much as we could hold without bothering to spit out the seeds. Suddenly our feast was interrupted by the barking of a dog. We grabbed our cans and acted extremely busy when the farmer and his dog walked toward us, watching how we took off the bugs and looked for eggs on the backsides of the leaves. Searching the ground for possible cherry seeds, he could not find what we had swallowed. Bending down too far urged the half-chewed fruits with seeds to return. Before the farmer left he praised us for doing such a good job and allowed us to take a handful home. We thanked him and after finishing the field, stuffed our apron pockets full of cherries and walked uphill, feeling most miserable.

It was late afternoon when I arrived home. My toes were aching from shoes that I had received from the American Red Cross. They must have once belonged to someone with slimmer feet than mine. I took them off to see my new blisters. Relieved and barefooted I walked silently upstairs. While passing our landlady's bedroom door on the second floor, I noticed the new paint job of green and gold—the traditional colors of the once royal family that lived six hundred years ago within these walls. The extremely large keyholes in the doors had turned our landlady into the famous "keyhole spy." Suddenly I remembered the beautiful black cherries still resting in my apron pocket. What a perfect timing for a second revenge! I squeezed one into the keyhole. It was for all the years I endured her hate and cursing. The next cherry was for all the victims she had spied on and caused troubles and embarrassments. And the last and biggest cherry was for all the times I had fallen down the dark staircase because she removed the light bulbs.

Going upstairs, I looked one more time at the door to see what a perfect job I had done. The dark red juice ran down over the still wet green and gold paint.

The following day I found out that the entire lock had been replaced because they could not manage to get out the seeds and the door had to be repainted. I was positive the landlady suspected I, she just could not prove it because many children came to see the doctor who had his apartment and office on the same floor.

FIRE IN THE CASTLE
AND THANKSGIVING

Mother had finally found a factory job in one of our neighboring villages. Working the evening shift, she took the train and came home after midnight. Being all alone in this spooky place I had the habit of lighting a candle and placing it on an old wooden U.S. Army C-ration box, which we used as a shelf, covered with a hand-knitted doily. It gave me enough light after I turned off the ceiling light at the door, to hurry and jump onto the army folding bed. After saying my prayers I would blow out the candle, which I had placed on the shelf behind my pillow. Next I would pull my quilt over my head to prevent hearing the whistling of the wind, birds in the chimney and strange sounds in the walls, hallway and nearby attics.

One night, hearing an unfamiliar noise, I pulled the cover up before I had blown out the candle. Feeling safe after praying, I fell asleep. I woke to my mother shaking me. Noticing she had been crying, I asked her what had happened. She was still wearing her overcoat, holding her purse and kept saying, "Praise God, praise the Lord!" I sat up and could not believe what I saw. The candle had burned down, igniting and burning up the almost-full matchbox next to it. The large flame had completely burned up one of my dolls, which had been sitting on one side of the candleholder but only burned part of the dress of the second doll sitting on the other side. A large hole was burned into the doily and the C-Ration box making a long trail down to the pillow where I had placed my head. When I asked Mother if she had put out the fire, she assured me she had found it being put out as she walked in. We both thanked God with tears for His wonderful protection, believing He had sent an angel to put out the flames.

During harvest season was our big holiday called Thanksgiving. For many days the schoolchildren gathered all kinds of fruits, vegetables and potatoes to display in baskets around the altar of our church. Most people who did not grow anything gave money.

On Thanksgiving we girls lined up in pairs of two wearing white dresses and a wreath in our hair, holding a fruit-filled basket while walking slowly into the church. When the organ played we sang our harvest song "We plow and we sow the seeds into the ground, but developing and growing is in the Hands of God." After the service the minister would gather all we had to hand out to the needy in the three villages where he preached. Providing and sharing with the poor would become a great blessing for the next harvest and for the lives of every giver.

Besides this holiday our village had its very own traditional "thanksgiving." It was in memory of a certain time in German history. It started when a Catholic monk, Martin Luther, began to translate the Bible from Latin into the German language to give all people the opportunity to read God's Word. He pointed out the many wrong teachings of his church according to the scripture. This ended up in a war between Catholics and Lutherans. The killing of the followers of Martin Luther, burning their farms and homes, lasted thirty years until the Swedish king Gustav Adolf used his army to help the Lutherans and finally end this religious battle. Near and far church bells would ring as a sign of peace. This village had kept up the tradition each day at four p.m. to ring the bells for a short time. The first time we heard it was when Mother and I shopped at the grocery store. Because all heads bowed for a silent prayer we thought someone important had died. After we noticed it was repeating each day, we began to ask questions and found out that by bowing their heads, people paid a tribute to all who had suffered for those thirty years. Beside the bell ringing being a heart-filled tradition, it was also a good sign for people in the forest and fields to know what time it was.

THE HOME FOR CHILDREN

Mother had to have surgery. To be in good hands, our pastor arranged for me to spend this time in a Lutheran Home for Children. The day of my arrival a missionary had a slide show presenting his work in a faraway country called "Africa." While the pictures were flashing over the screen, he had chosen to play the song "Fairest Lord Jesus." It showed how Lutheran sisters had dedicated their lives to Jesus, working among the poor, caring for the sick, teaching the children and using the Word of God to give people hope and a purpose for living. It was an evening that put my heart on fire for Jesus and I planned to become one of those wonderful sisters who shared Gods' love.

The joy of my new discovery for my future only lasted for one week until I was called to the office to see the head sister. This elderly sister who had welcomed me with open arms and promised my mother I would have a wonderful time, now threw an open letter into my face. She accused me of lying to my mother, writing her they would not dress me warm enough. All Mother had written was for me to dress warm because snow had been reported in some parts of the country. And all I had written was how much I liked the place and the new school. I did not get a chance to defend myself and while she opened the door for me to leave, she screamed that from now on all my mail would be opened.

Since this was a home for boys only, I had to stay with the small group of preschool children, half boys and half girls. We all slept in a very large room called "mouse hole." Everyone had a nice small bed, only mine was a baby bed with a fence. Being eleven and very tall for my age I had to pull my knees up to my face to fit, without being able to turn. I thought about the floor, but it was too hard and too cold because the second floor was not being heated. Christina, a young and very friendly lady who took care of the preschoolers, apologized about my bed, but I told her not to worry because it would only be for a short time. Soon all the little "mice" looked at me as an older sister. Each day I came home from school all of them tried to talk to me at the same time. To make them happy I waited until bedtime to tell them a story. After Christina finished her prayer and told us to be silent and sleep, she turned off the light and closed the door. I waited until the staircase light shining through the opening under our door went out to start with one of my favorite fairy tales. Everyone was excited and every night I had to tell a new story.

Breakfast, as well as lunch, I had to eat with the boys in a large dining hall. I had to sit at the table with the two sisters. The younger one, who was taking care of all the boys, had a very proud and unfriendly face. I was always glad to leave the table and in the morning line up with the school boys to receive our food for recess. Sister Elfriede stood by the door handing out one thick slice of bread to each boy leaving. When it was my turn she searched in her large bowl to find a small piece. Just because I was a girl did not make me less hungry, besides I was taller than most boys my age. It was written all over her face that I did not fit into this place. Feeling hurt I only whispered a short "thanks" like all the boys did and on my way out gave it away. She must have watched me and told me the next day I had to keep it. Not to upset her any further, I kept it only until I was out of her sight, knowing I had arranged to trade my knowledge in writing and talent in drawing for recess food.

The rule was that anyone coming home late for lunch was not allowed to eat. Whenever it happened, the hungry boys hung around the kitchen area depending on the pity of the hired help. I usually kept my pockets stuffed with hazelnuts, rosehips or sour berries that were growing on the roadside along the steep hill. Later these bushes became a real lifesaver the time it had snowed heavily all night and morning. When we left the school all we could see was snow. The wind had drifted it against the mountain and covered our road. Only some of the branches of the bushes I picked from told us where the road was. Poking into the snow we carefully made a trail up the hill, bringing everyone home safe and sound. Though we all were late, we were allowed to eat lunch and I had the feeling it was based on the fact no one had bothered to come and help us.

Watching the boys through the window having snowball fights made me want to join them. It brought back memories of my home in East Germany when my brothers made a large castle from snow bricks. I could have been a big help to these boys but was not allowed to join them per Sister Elfriede. To be happy and useful I had to wait until night when the "mice" begged me for another story. Again we watched the staircase light and waited for it to go off to continue. I was in the middle of a fairy tale when suddenly a large shadow bent over me and hit me so hard across my face my cheeks were burning. In the moonlight coming through the window I could tell it wore the bonnet and a long wide skirt. It made a fast turn and silently disappeared into the dark. Everything had happened so fast without a sound of the door or any footsteps. We all knew it could only have been Sister Elfriede. It made an end to our secret time of story hour.

BATHTIME

Each Saturday was bathtime in the "mouse hole." It was the only time when the little black stove with the long pipe was filled with wood and coal to heat up our large bedroom. A large tub was placed on two benches pushed together standing close by the stove, next to the door. Because I was the oldest in this group, I was first in line so that I could be of help to dry everyone off after Christina had given each a bath. We were told to take off our nightgown and leave it on our beds, but being eleven and showing visible signs of being a female, kept holding it to cover my chest while walking and climbing into the tub. Christina smiled and made a remark understanding my embarrassment. While she was sponging me off, Sister Elfriede came walking in, leaving the door wide open to discuss something important. Soon a group of boys that had gathered outside the door watching me were told to leave by one of the older boys named Helmut. Apologizing without looking at me, he shut the door. Looking at my red face I could tell how satisfied the sister was, knowing what she had done to me. She reminded me of the castle's dragon lady, the only difference was, she wore a holy robe. The next time I passed by Helmut, I gave him a little smile to thank him for being polite.

Shortly before Christmas I found the dining hall off limits to enter. Because the door was partially open, I stood and listened. Sister Elfriede was practicing Christmas songs while Helmut played the piano for her. She had a beautiful voice and picked all the songs that were my favorites. If I would have not felt her horns that certain night I could have assumed she was an angel. When she was not singing she was talking and laughing, acting more like a girl my age as if it had

171

slipped her mind who she was supposed to be. I had never seen her being that way to any other boy, especially the one who had to share our
breakfast table. Almost every day he had been late with red eyes looking as if he had been crying. One of the boys had mentioned he was
known as "bed wetter" and punished each time. I felt sorry for him.

Many times walking down the long hallway, I noticed she
always had Helmut carry something for her. That's when I heard
"Thank you Sister Elfriede," "Please - sorry- how wonderful" and
"Of course, Sister Elfriede" until I could hear his words echo in my
memory. He seemed to be her personal pet, following her and adoring her like a lonely puppy.

It was on a Friday after lunch when I asked Christina if I could
decorate the big dollhouse for Christmas while the "mice" took their
afternoon nap. She agreed and told me where to go to find the things
I needed. Passing by the dining hall I could see the "Do Not Enter"
sign hanging on the doorknob, which was used for the boys' bathtime. Remembering how Sister Elfriede had embarrassed me sitting
in the tub by leaving the door wide open so everyone could view
me, gave me the idea to steam up her anger. Spilling some of the
milk in front of the door, which was left over from lunch, I turned
the sign around before I walked in. It was extremely noisy with boys
sitting at the long tables playing games, some undressing and lining
up for bathtime. No one seemed to pay attention to me as I walked
toward the broom closet. Sister Elfriede looked funny wearing a long
butcher shop apron with her sleeves rolled up and her arms deep in
the tub to sponge off one of the boys. Leaving with mop and bucket,
I took my time until she noticed me. Her face was dark red with
anger, screaming at me like the dragon lady, only this one wore a
holy robe. I felt sorry for Helmut having to climb into that tub to be
washed by her. It made me remember how my brother Martin, being
Helmut's age while living in the refugee camp in Austria, made sure
no one looked at him, not even my mother, and hid behind a sheet
while washing up.

GOING HOME

The big flame in my heart, to dedicate my life and become one of those wonderful Lutheran sisters, was burning lower with every day. Each time I came close to Sister Elfriede I could feel an unpleasant tension. Though she showed up again in the morning during our bathtime, she was out of luck finding me in the tub with my back facing the door.

Finally it was Christmas. Because I was ordered to stay with the schoolchildren, Sister Elfriede had to help Christina dress and walk the preschoolers to church. The older boys, who were in charge, lined us up in the yard to make sure we were all present. It was already dark and snowing again. We were split up into smaller groups to go down the snowy hill. I felt someone pulling my woolen hat over my ears and turned around. It was Helmut, who took my hand saying he did not want me to get lost. Silently we walked behind the last group. Though he was only two years older than I, his hand was a lot larger with a tight grip. I closed my eyes and felt like I was walking with Martin through the snow in East Germany and across the meadows of Austria while he held my hand. Helmut, who had noticed it, told me to keep my eyes open. When I told him I had been thinking about my brother, who I missed, it led into a long conversation until we had reached the church.

Because many of the little children who had been sitting in that cold church waiting for us started to cry, the Pastor kept the service short. While Christina and Sister Elfriede took them back home, we went to the school auditorium for the Nativity play and to sing. On the way home I heard all about how Helmut had lost both of his parents at an early age and grew up in this children home, missing out on family life and the feeling of being loved. I had dropped my plan to tell him all about Sister Elfriede but when he asked me why I had walked into the dining hall during bathtime, I told him about my silent battle with her. To my surprise he thanked me for all I told him.

After our breakfast on Christmas Day, we all had to return to our bedrooms and wait until the ringing of the bell for the celebration. This gave me plenty of time for more fairy tales while everyone listened being covered up. After the bell went off doors were slammed, and children ran until it felt as if the staircase was breaking from everyone lining up on it and in the corridor. When the dining hall opened up I looked at the most beautiful tree I had ever seen, decorated with little red apples, silvery walnuts, colored iced gingerbread and long icicles hanging on large branches holding lighted candles. While Sister Elfriede sang like an angel, Helmut played the piano as we listened while sitting at white-covered tables sipping hot cocoa. Our gift consisted of a large plate filled with apples, different kinds of nuts, cookies and some candies. But my greatest Christmas gift was my memory of Helmut's smile, feeling the warmth of his hand through my mittens and the feeling of "peace on earth and good will" toward Sister Elfriede. The mail I should have received at Christmas was handed out to me a few days later. It was a letter from Mother saying she would be home soon and that a package was on its way from one of my aunts containing a hand-knitted sweater and chocolate, which I split with all the "mice" and Christina.

The following week I was asked to go to the main office to see the head sister. Wondering what it was about I found my suitcase sitting next to the door. She helped me put on my coat and told me my mother was waiting at home. I had my answer why she suddenly was so nice to me, after she told me there would be no goodbyes to prevent a lot of unnecessary tears. Not understanding nor believing what I heard, one of the kitchen helpers grabbed my suitcase to take me to the train. The elderly sister shook my hand while smiling and wishing me a safe trip home. Thinking about the "mice," Christina and Helmut I could not keep my tears inside. For almost an hour we followed a snowplow to the train station. The lady helped me board the train and stayed with me until it left. It gave her a chance to warm up and share a few of her own ill feelings toward the sisters. Mother was waiting for me at the train station and I had a lot to tell her. One thing I was sure of, I would never become a sister wearing a "holy robe." That's when Mother smiled, saying we can serve Jesus without wearing a robe of the church and that Jesus loved us and had a white robe waiting on the end of our lives.

MAKING UP AND A BAD JOKE

My classmates could not wait to hear all about the "Home for Boys" where I had spent several months. We chose the recess when our needlecraft teacher used extra time to flirt with the Catholic priest. While one of the girls stood at the window keeping an eye on her, everyone crowded around me to listen. It was so quiet one could have heard a needle drop. Putting my story into a nut shell, I was finished when our spy reported she was on her way up. That gave everyone enough time to sit at their desk acting busy embroidering when she walked through the door. Smiling, she shook her head in disbelief how well behaved and quiet we had been.

After I studied to make up for all the subjects I had missed in school while I had been away, some of the boys in our class came up with a perfect joke. Our pastor had been elected for an alarm clock hunt. He was aged and grey haired and did his utmost to fill us with knowledge of the Word of God. But because he was very kind, he was less respected than the other teachers. Everyone was asked to bring their alarm clock the following day for our Bible lesson.

The next morning in school I found my classmates busy running around, hiding their alarm clocks and setting them several minutes apart to ring. I apologized, explaining why we did not need nor own one. Our dragon lady woke up her house maid every morning at five a.m. She sat her monster clock on our staircase and let it ring for a half an hour. The rest of the day the clock from the steeple told us what time it was.

Exactly at eight our pastor entered our classroom. While he spoke the morning blessing the first alarm clock went off. Wondering what it was about he followed the noise to the many jackets and overcoats that hung against our classroom wall. We watched him search to find the clock hiding inside the sleeve of a coat, when the next alarm rang on the opposite side of the room. While these two clocks were still ringing others went off and watching our pastor running from place to place to end this evil, caused everyone to bend over laughing. The ringing of many clocks and the screaming and laughing of the students was a concert that even began to irritate some of the boys who had invented this game. The joke had now backfired. Our pastor finally gave up, with his hands and voice shaking he uttered something no one could hear, grabbed his briefcase, Bible and left. Suddenly the good time everyone wanted to have was now over. Half of the class was still talking and laughing, others worried about being reported to the principal and others felt somehow guilty. I, too, could not help laughing in the beginning but soon was aware we had miscalculated. Looking down from our classroom window, I could see him walking across the schoolyard and felt sorry for what we had done. I felt as though we all had committed a crime. Telling myself I had no alarm clock did not change anything, I had been part of the gang, part of hurting someone. Everyone was happy we had managed to have a whole hour to talk and play and discuss what kind of punishment we would receive once the principal heard about it. But since our pastor was kind and forgiving, nothing happened.

MY LAST SCHOOL YEAR

I wanted to make Mother happy to finally change the ugly "F" I got each year in needlecraft. Each time my teacher handed me my yearly report card he shook his head and said he could not believe why someone that was an "A" and "B" student could be so bad. After embroidery we picked up hand sewing. Our last project was supposed to be a flannel nightgown. I had several that my aunts had given me as Christmas gifts and Mother suggested that I ask the teacher if I could use the same pattern, only make a blouse instead. It would help us to purchase less fabric. To my surprise our teacher agreed and even smiled at me. This gave me hope and with Mother being a seamstress, I was sure to make a better grade this time.

I worked extra hard, knowing it would be our last report card and of great importance for our future, in case I would choose the profession of tailoring or arts and crafts, like my aunt Elfriede. After I hand sewed my beautiful blouse it was much admired by all my classmates. The hot pink fabric full of white daisies made all the flannel nightgowns look dull. Even Mother said I had done a good job.

Finally it was time for our report cards to be handed out. I had the usual excellent grades, but in sewing and needlecraft nothing however had changed. Everyone was sure the teacher had made a mistake. Even Mother could not believe it and took me and my report card to confront the teacher. With a big smile on her face she explained that I had not followed the rules to use flannel fabric like the rest of the girls. I could tell how upset Mother was and remembered her confronting the Nazi teacher of our hometown who made her walk out of the classroom like a beaten dog. But that was then, this was now.

Our next trip was to the principal's office. Mother insisted I should have been graded for my sewing and not for the kind of fabric I used. Cowardly, he took a short look at my blouse saying he could not see anything wrong with it, but then he was not an "expert" in sewing. To change the subject, he informed us that our government gave every refugee child three free years of commercial school and since I was excellent in writing, my "F" in needlecraft was of no importance. I could tell Mother was not happy with his answer, but it was a way to solve the problem.

I had passed my test for another three years of school. But each time I looked into the display window of a yarn shop admiring the beautiful creations I felt sad, knowing my "F" had locked the door to a profession I would have liked.

Our village school located next to the castle had spoiled me. Now I had to get up at five a.m. to catch the smoke-filled and over-crowded train Monday through Friday to the city of Nuernberg. Next was a long trolley ride that made me feel like I was a sardine packed in a can. By the time I came home it was late afternoon, leaving me little time for homework. It made me feel like a butterfly in captivity. Missing the beauty and silence that only nature could give me I grabbed a blanket and my English schoolbook to study on a hill behind the village. From there I had a beautiful view into the valley with fields, meadows, brooks and trails until it met the dark pine forest with distant villages, until it met the evening sky. There I made the acquaintance of Walter, a most handsome young man. Identifying both of his dogs I knew he was our new forest ranger's son who had come home for the holiday to visit his parents. Introducing himself as a student of law living in a faraway city, we had a delightful evening until the moonlight reminded us it was time to go home. To him, I was the smart little country girl in pigtails trying to study English, and to me he was someone who had stepped out of a dream, enjoying his company and never asking any questions about who I was or where I came from. For the first time in my life I felt equal to mankind being treated with kindness and respect. With our good sense of humor we both were a perfect match and were sad to see the evening end. But it made me happy to hear him ask me if he could see me again next time. And while he enjoyed seeing me blush, he took a small twig from the hedge of jasmine, which covered the garden wall of the ranger residence, gave it to me and wished me sweet dreams.

Each time Walter came home for a visit, we met on the hill or strolled through the meadows and forest until dark. He had touched my heart in a special way and I caught myself daydreaming about him. Being only fourteen, it was possible he saw in me the little sister he never had, but the instinct of a woman told me he was much aware of reality. I had fallen in love and lived on wishful thinking that someday in the future he would turn our evenings into a lifetime romance. But my wonderful dream came to a bitter ending during our annual village festival. Elisabeth asked me if I would like to join her at the dance. But I refused to go, not because this dance hall had bad memories of the time we arrived as refugees, but because I only wanted to dance in the arms of Walter. When my sister returned the next morning I found out what a terrible mistake I had made by keeping my evenings with Walter a secret and not telling him I had a beautiful older sister. Unexpectedly, he had come for a visit and spent the time together that broke my heart and crushed my dreams. After that night, each time he came home to visit his parents, I stayed home. I watched him from my window, looking out of the ranger's mansion for my appearance to go to the hill until dark and later. I never meant to disappoint him, but I felt too hurt and too proud to confront him about what had happened. At the same time I felt guilty and ashamed for being young and living on wishful dreaming.

It was several years later when I accidentally ran into Walter again. We were both taking the evening train home. He seemed surprised and happy to see me and could not believe how much I had changed. Two years had matured me by changing my pigtails into curls and putting a ring on my finger. He was shocked and disappointed when he learned I was engaged to a U.S. paratrooper. When he friendly warned me that soldiers are known to break young girl hearts, I was reminded he was the first one who broke mine without knowing it. Smiling, while hiding the pain I remembered, I assured him that my heart was made out of steel.

It all happened a long time ago. Opening my old English schoolbook I found the small twig of faded jasmine Walter had given me when we first met. I had to admit how right he was saying soldiers break young girl hearts. My heart had been broken many times until I found that special someone, whose gentle smile found a way to mend it.

And now, just like the twig of jasmine has lost its color, texture and fragrance, I feel the loss of youth, strength and ideals, but never the precious memories that are engraved forever in my heart.

In the train with Walter.